IMMORTAL HEXES

VAMPIRE MATES

AMELIA HUTCHINS

IMMORTAL HEXES

Authored By: Amelia Hutchins
Cover Art Design: Simply Defined Art
Copy edited by: E & F Indie Services
Edited by: E & F Indie Services
Published in (United States of America)
10 9 8 7 6 5 4 3 2 1

DEDICATION

This one is for the girls who have been through hell and somehow manage to stay standing. To the ones who don't see themselves as beautiful anymore. You're beautiful even if you don't see it. It is okay to fall down, or to take your time as you rise, but rise you shall you beautiful mess. This one is for us, the battered and broken, and the wounded warriors who looks into the mirror and sees the horror that she survived, and yet still manages to smile. Let your shine out, remember to smile, and never, ever think you're not worth fighting for. Sparkle you beautiful bitch, because what didn't kill you will eventually make you stronger, and become your armor.

ALSO BY AMELIA HUTCHINS

ALSO BY AMELIA HUTCHINS

Midnight Coven Books
Forever Immortal
Immortal Hexes
Witches, coming soon

Upcoming Series

A Crown of Ashes

Fae Hunter Series

If you're following the series for the Fae Chronicles, Elite Guards, and Monsters, reading order is as follows:

Fighting Destiny
Taunting Destiny
Escaping Destiny
Seducing Destiny
A Demon's Dark Embrace
Playing with Monsters
Unraveling Destiny
Sleeping with Monsters
Claiming the Dragon King
Oh, Holy Knight
Becoming his Monster
The Winter Court
A Demon's Plaything
If She's Wicked
Embracing Destiny *Coming Soon*

Warning!

Stop!! Read the warning below before purchasing this book.

Warning:

This is a brutal story of coming back from being tortured. Avery is a very strong character who has endured pain, torture, and a love that has always haunted her. This story is dark, and shows the struggle of how a victim sees and feels after they've lived through hell. It shows her struggle to become whole again.

Second Warning in case the first didn't scare you: This book is **dark**. It's **sexy**, hot, and **intensely twisted**. The author is human, you are as well. Is the book perfect? It's as perfect as I could make it. Are there mistakes? Probably, then again, even **New York Times top published** books have minimal mistakes because like me, they have **human editors**. There are words in this book that won't be found in the **standard dictionary**, because they were created to set the stage for a paranormal-urban fantasy world. Different words are common in paranormal books and give better description to the action in the story than can be found in standard dictionaries. They are **intentional** and not mistakes.

About the hero: chances are you may **not** fall instantly in **love** with him, that's because **I don't write men you instantly love**; you grow to love them. I don't believe in **instant-love**. I write flawed, raw, caveman-like **alpha-holes** that eventually let you see their redeeming qualities. They are **aggressive**, **alpha-holes**, one step above a caveman when we meet them. You may *not* even like him by the time you finish this book, but I promise you will **love** him by the **end** of this **series**.

Warning! (Cont'd)

About the heroine: There is a chance, that you might think she's a bit naïve or weak, but then again who starts out as a badass? Badasses are a product of growth and I am going to put her through **hell**, and you get to watch **her** come up **swinging** every time I knock her on her ass. That's just how I do things. How she reacts to the set of circumstances she is put through, may not be how you as the reader, or I as the author would react to that same situation. Everyone reacts differently to circumstances and how Avery responds to her challenges, is how I see her as a character and as a person.

I don't write love stories: I write fast paced, knock you on your ass, make you sit on the edge of your seat wondering what happens in the next kind of books. If you're looking for cookie cutter romance, this isn't for you. If you can't handle the ride, *un-buckle your seatbelt and get out of the roller-coaster car now*. **If not, you've been warned.** If nothing outlined above bothers you, carry on and **enjoy the ride!**

IMMORTAL HEXES

VAMPIRE MATES

CHAPTER ONE

THE RECKONING

Thunder rumbled above the training grounds where students relentlessly practiced calling flames into their palms. My gaze drifted up, lingering on the clouds as I watched lightning strike in the distance, followed by another deafening grumble from the sky in the mountains we hid in. Storms were a dime a dozen here, which was one of the draws to this particular area. The allure of sanctuary within the mountains of the Inland Northwest brought me to this place of turbulent weather offering me peace.

Watching Clara, I frowned as her slim shoulders slumped in defeat, nary a flicker of a flame filling her palm. Out of the bloodlines present this year at the academy, hers was the lowest among them. This school, this training facility, catered to the oldest bloodlines of witches in the world. Most of the students belonged to lines dating back to the original witches. I'd taught the witches and warlocks to wield their darkness, to balance it with the light, for over one hundred and fifty years; long before the ground we stood upon had ever been inhabited by the English.

A few feet from me, Johnny watched Flora as she pulled a large amount of energy into the palm of her hand with a sly smile on her lips. Her father was a high witch, one who sat on the council. Roger had pulled strings to get her into the academy; he'd demanded it, even though her mother was a mundane human. Her mother's blood had merely watered down Flora's, making her magic unpredictable. Studying the sweat that beaded her brow, mixed with the lines of concentration on her face, I matched Clara's frown. I whispered a spell, gaining control of the energy Flora had pulled to her so that when she lost control, no one was harmed.

Two minutes after I'd taken control from her, she screamed out a warning as she whimpered in pain. Her eyes bulged, moving from the now floating energy ball to me, knowing I'd taken control of her magic and now held it for her.

"I had it under control! Why do you continue to mess with me when I am far better than everyone else?" she hissed, staring me down, her pretty blue eyes filling with fire as her ire rose.

"Because you didn't have it under control," I replied softly, watching her aura as it turned black with red etching. "The lesson is about control; not to show how powerful one is. We don't care how much energy you pull up, only that what you bring forth is controlled. Try it again. This time only bring up a flame, and make sure you have absolute control over it."

"You know who my father is and what he can do to you, right? He doesn't think of you highly considering your past deeds and why you are here in the first place.

You are the whore who slept with a vampire, after all, are you not?" she laughed coldly, her eyes filling with liquid blue flames as she squared her shoulders as the few witchlings she considered friends laughed and waited for my reply.

"Are you asking if it is true? It is. I lost my entire coven and family to the Black Death, and while I lay in an alley dying of it myself, Conner, the son of Grigori Halverson and King of the England Vampires, saved me. He dug me out of the trash and saved my life. For days, I waited and prayed to Hecate to send me help or take my soul, neither of which happened. So I remained with him, drinking his blood to stave off the plague that continued to come back once the blood eased from my system. He saved me, and I loved him for it. Had he not saved me, I'd have perished without getting word to the other covens that not even the strongest bloodlines were immune to the Black Death. His saving me also saved thousands of witches from intervening to save the humans. Had they tried to help them as my coven had done, we would have become extinct, because they would have tried and perished by doing so. Did I fuck him? Yes, but not until years after I lived with him in their hive. I was guarded by him, cherished. He never asked to wield my wild magic for his gain. After five years of living among them, I offered him my virtue, and he alone fucked me.

"Do you know how turbulent the world was in the 1600s? We were at war with their kind, and I was alone within the enemy's nest. I was abandoned by our kind because to come for me would have been death, which the vampires knew, and yet Conner refused to allow them to exploit me. So, there I stayed, and yes, I fell in love with my enemy, and I gave him everything I had, except my magic. I never wielded a single spell against our kind while I was with them. Others who had befallen a similar fate either turned to the dark arts to escape or were fucked to literal death as the vampires drained them. Tell me, Flora, what would you have done to survive? Would you have fought them, knowing that they would just as soon murder you and end your life, or find one who could help keep you safe from an entire nest of ancient beings that wanted you dead?" I stared her down with the fire of a thousand memories rushing through my mind.

"Couldn't you have killed them?" Joshua asked as he kicked a rock beneath his foot, watching me as I frowned.

"Back then, no. I was only thirteen summers when he found me and I was alone in a pile of dead bodies, dying of the very plague that had killed my coven. I had very little control over my magic. I was barely into my training when my coven walked into that sick house to save those who needed our aid. My mother, Ilsa Cheveron, was one of the strongest witches alive at that time, but to train in those days could only be done during a full moon or eclipse since the discovery of a witch would result in being burned at the stake. So with very little control or training, I was unarmed and outmanned. Can anyone tell me the rules of engagement for the early and mid-1600s?"

"I'm sure fucking the enemy wasn't one of them," Flora snorted as she crossed her arms over her ample breasts, staring at me pointedly.

"Survive and secure the bloodlines," Clara said over the laughter of Flora's cronies. She looked at me for direction, and I nodded for her to continue. "In those days, we were fewer because of the war between our kind and the vampires, and to survive was of the utmost priority. If you were captured by the enemy, you were to survive and endure until the covens learned of it and found a way to get you back. Bloodlines were pure, and the older ones were treasured, and since Miss Avery is a Cheveron witch, she'd have been under stricter rules than others. She would be told to do whatever it took to survive until escape was possible."

"And I did. I am still here, am I not?" I pointed out as the assembly of teenagers watched me. "Now, if you're finished with me, can we get back to training you? Because had I known how to control my magic, I would have been able to escape their hive and make my way to the coven within England instead of playing a part to survive them," I said, exhaling the breath that seemed to falter as memories of that time plagued me.

"How long were you with him?" Flora asked softly, her anger deflating as the others stopped fueling it.

"For a very long time," I admitted.

"You've watched the world grow and change, and yet you stay here, teaching us, why?" Joshua asked.

"Look at your friends, look at their faces. Now imagine living without them. Watching them age until they become ashes, scattered upon the wind as they are returned to the earth. I have lived for over three hundred years, and I have watched almost everyone that I have ever considered a friend die. All but one has been reclaimed by the earth, and she's here with me. I have watched the world grow and change, Kings crowned and slaughtered. I have been a witness as governments were toppled to ruin. I have watched covens die out because they chose to keep their children close to their home, and here...here I can help teach you how to survive. So why am I here? To teach you not to end up as I have," I chided softly as my chest tightened.

It wasn't why I was here. I was here because I was hunted; I'd killed a King. I killed and an entire hive of royalty when I'd escaped; that wasn't something the vampires would allow to go unanswered, and we all knew it. So, I hid in these mountains and continued to survive.

Sooner or later, Conner would come for me, and when he did, I knew he'd show no mercy. Not that he had it back then, but with me, he'd always been gentle. I'd chosen these mountains for the serenity long before they were discovered by man. I raised the academy from a tiny wooden house to a school with over three hundred students at times. I'd hidden here to escape the world, to hide the shame of my crimes from the covens, but also because when I'd come here, man had yet to discover it. No humans meant no vampires, because, without humans, they would starve to death.

"That can't be easy," Flora admitted.

"Death is part of life, be thankful you have the option. Now, everyone, back to learning how to control the magic within you," I said as I turned, eyeing Laura, who shook her head at my story.

"I wish the council members would learn to hold their tongues on our histories," she said, moving to my side and we watched the witchlings once again try to call their magic to them. "Life would be so much simpler here if they did."

"Look at the sky," I said. Gazing up into the black clouds, I narrowed my eyes on the sun as the moon sat before it. "Is there an eclipse planned?" The only person who could create such an event was a witch, and a damn powerful one at that. I could barely make the sun disappear, but to manage a full eclipse? That took a long time to plan and an even longer time to spell the world to heed the magic.

"Not that I was made aware," she stated, shielding her eyes as she stared up at the dark sky. "That's rather strange since it would be a cause for celebration. You'd think we'd have felt it coming."

"Clara, focus!" I shouted as she lost her footing. I captured her energy ball before it slammed into Flora. I expelled a shaky breath as I turned to speak to Laura.

"That was close," she stated, shivering against the reality of what had almost happened. "What do you think is blocking Clara? She's been here for over two years and has yet to control even a whisper of magic."

"She is the only thing holding herself back. She fears her magic, and she should. Out of everyone here, she holds the strongest power, yet she is terrified of it. It's rather strange if you consider her bloodline compared to the others."

"And Johnny and Flora, you do know they've gone further into their relationship and have begun sneaking out and fucking beneath the bleachers, right?" she laughed.

"I'm aware, but it is only our job to teach them to control the magic, not their unlimited hormones. It's in the contract. If she becomes pregnant, her father would rejoice and welcome the child. Johnny's grandmother, on the other hand, would see it cast off and denounced. Again, that isn't our problem. They come to learn, and we teach them what no one else can. What happens between them is on them and is their parents' problem," I muttered as lightning crashed against a tree beside us.

The smell of burnt wood and singed leaves filled the air as I stared at where the bolt had struck. The sky still rumbling and clapping loudly above us and everyone ceased training at once. My magic grasped for theirs, halting their energy from being expelled at one another. "Fuck," I uttered as their magic fought against mine. "Laura, help me," I whispered painfully, my chest constricting with the effort it took to gain control of it all. Her hand touched my shoulder, and the pressure eased as, together, we sheltered them from the magic they'd been distracted from noticing.

"Something isn't right, can you feel that?" she asked, but I couldn't do anything but hold the magic as, one by one, I blinked it out of existence and back into the leyline from which our magic originated.

Once the magic was returned, I swallowed hard and looked up, watching as the sun began to disappear behind the moon. Day turned to night, spreading darkness through the meadow in which we stood, exposed. My breathing hitched as I dropped my stare to peer around the edge of the meadow.

"We need to get them to safety, now," I whispered through the heaviness of my tongue. I'd seen this once before. "This is not a drill, inside now!" I shouted to be heard over the howling wind that came out of nowhere.

"Everyone inside!" Laura clapped her hands, clearing the air around us from the screaming of the wind so we could be heard. "I want you all to get inside immediately. Something is wrong, come with me," Laura urged, turning to me as I stood still, locked into place, staring at the shadows at the edge of the meadow. "What is it, Avery?"

"He's here," I mumbled as fear snaked up my spine to wrap around my throat. "He's found me; the devil is here." My heart fluttered as it began to beat faster. The sound of it in my ears drowned out the howling of the wind as I stared at the tallest figure that stepped out of the shadows of the trees. "Laura, go!"

"Not without you, Avery. We can make it," she stated, but we both knew we wouldn't. I looked up at the last remaining sliver of the sun, the only thing holding them in the shadows, and turned to face her.

"You will go and get to safety and call the council to come save me. They will demand my release, for the secrets you and I hold against them are too many for them to allow us to be captured by their enemies. The students need you, and he won't leave here without me. I know him, he isn't a murderous bastard, and he won't hurt them if I go with him. You have to trust me on this. Now go!"

She took off at a run to where the students were still milling through the door, and I called forth magic to embrace me, to give me enough strength to give them a fighting chance against the monsters that waited for the last sliver of light to be swallowed by the moon. The moment it was, the entire meadow held its breath as the only sound was my ragged breathing. Laura and the students wouldn't make it inside before they reached us, and that knowledge slithered around my heart, tightening its hold as if it had been placed into a vise. I swallowed down anger as I watched Royal move to catch Laura while she ushered the students into the school. The entire world seemed to stop as he ripped her back by her hair and turned her to face me. My magic began to unravel as I opened my mouth to whisper the spell that would end his life. A hand covered my mouth as a hard body pressed against my back. Another arm snaked around my chest, holding me in place. Power sizzled over my flesh with awareness as butterflies erupted in my stomach, wings fluttering as the scent of masculinity hit my nose.

"Hello, waif, I've missed you," a deep, husky baritone uttered against my ear as his heated breath fanned the shell of my ear. "Whisper one fucking word of magic, and I will slaughter everyone here, do you understand me? Nod if you do," he growled.

I nodded and felt his hand moving away from my mouth. Turning slowly, I gazed up into violet-blue eyes that I knew as well as my own. His thick, dark hair was windswept, wild and untamed as he stared into my eyes as if he was looking through me, to my soul. I opened my mouth to speak, and his eyes dropped to my lips as a dark brow lifted in warning.

"Conner," I whispered thickly as my throat tightened with memories. I searched his eyes, shaking my head, preparing to beg him to release the students as they whimpered and cried with fear, their entrance being blocked by the undead.

"Did you think I would forget what you did? That

I wouldn't come for you and make you pay for it? No, I've never forgotten your treachery or the betrayal, and neither has anyone else, Avery," he chuckled as his hand came up to cup my cheek as if he intended to be gentle, but I knew better. There was nothing left of the gentle lover he'd once been. His fingers wrapped around my throat and a cruel smile spread over his generous mouth as he held me up. "I'm going to fucking wreck you, witch. When I finish with you, you're going to wish I'd left you in the garbage where I found you," he purred, his eyes watching as mine rounded with fear as my feet kicked nothing but air. He tossed me back, knocking the wind from my lungs as I landed on the hard ground. I turned over, and crawled to where Royal, Conner's brother, held Laura, his deadly fangs scraping over her exposed throat.

I opened my mouth to call forth the wind when his hands gripped my hair, and he pulled me back to where he knelt on his haunches. His other hand held my chin, biting into my flesh as he brushed his nose over my bare shoulder.

"You will watch her die with me so that you know what it feels like to have the people you love slaughtered."

"Conner, no, I will do anything. Please, please let them go, and I will do anything you want, just tell me what to do," I uttered through the pain and emotions that tore through me. Tears welled in my eyes as I watched Laura's lip quivering with the knowledge that she would suffer through what Royal would do to her. Tears slipped free, sliding down my cheek to touch his hand. My breathing was labored, my chest rising and falling with each second that ticked by. Crimson red blood dripped from Laura's neck where Royal had nicked her flesh. "Conner, please. Kill me, torture me, do whatever you want to me, but let them go."

"Like you did my family? Did you show them mercy?" he asked softly, and I stiffened as those memories replaced the ones that he and I had made so long ago.

Screaming erupted behind me, but I didn't dare try to rip my chin from his hold as Clara screamed and begged for help. How had I let this happen? How had I missed the magic that they used to turn day to night, and how the fuck was *he* holding it? Vampires couldn't wield magic, which meant he employed a very powerful witch. He released my jaw and turned me by his hold on my hair until I was forced to look over my shoulder at him.

"You want me to let her live? Make me believe you will do anything to ensure it happens," he snapped. I turned on my knees, wincing as rocks bit into them. My hands shook violently as I pushed his shirt up to access his flesh. My head dipped before I stared up at him, kissing his stomach as he watched me through hate-filled eyes. My hand pushed past the waistband of his pants, gripping his thick cock, and a whimper exploded from my lips as his arm snaked around me, pulling me roughly against him without warning. "Did you miss me, waif? Miss my touch, my cock, and my kisses?" he asked as heat banked in his eyes even though his smile remained cruel as his fingers bit into the flesh at the small of my back.

"No," I whispered, knowing it would piss him off,

and yet I wouldn't let him think I'd thought of him since he'd left me in the care of his father. "Not even a little bit, Conner," I smirked, working his cock as my insides liquefied to mush and wantonness.

"Mmm, judging by the wetness of your cunt I can smell, I don't believe you. I'm going to enjoy destroying you and listening to you beg me to do it," he laughed soundlessly as he ripped me up from the ground by my hair, forcing me to pull my hands from his pants as he did so. "Bring them both," he ordered.

"No, Conner," I whispered. "Me, use me. Let them remain here, they weren't a part of it."

"No, only one murderous bitch. It matters little to me if they live or die. I'm not afraid to wage war against the covens. They are coming with us so that when you step out of line, I can use them to show what I wish to do to you. Be a good girl, Avery, and don't make me murder your friends."

CHAPTER TWO

An entire week had gone by since we'd been captured, and I hadn't seen or heard from Conner. The small cell that the three of us had been tossed into smelled of mildew and decay, but judging by the corpse two cells over, we could end up staying here much longer. Clara cried in the corner as Laura tried to comfort her. I chewed my lip, ignoring them both while I paced the length of the cell, wondering when he would come for me.

"We need water, and soon," Laura said softly, her emerald green eyes holding mine as I blinked back tears of frustration.

"I don't think they care what we need," I pointed out as I rubbed my naked arms against the chill in the cell. Unlike Laura and me, Clara needed sustenance, and I was sure we were being neglected to make a point. Conner wanted me down here, wondering when he would come and fearing it. I knew his games because I'd watched him play them a million times before.

"She won't stop crying," Laura hissed as if Clara

couldn't hear us discussing her two feet away from where she sat huddled in a ball, rocking her lithe frame back and forth as sob after sob expelled from her lungs. "She's dehydrating herself, and we can't replenish it in here."

"No shit? I don't know what you expect me to do here. It isn't like he fucking cares if we die, or cares about me at all. If I ask him for water, I guarantee you, the answer will be no."

Screaming sounded from above us, and I eyed the ceiling irritably, hearing the men grunt as women called out in pleasure. They were celebrating my capture and had been since I'd been tossed into the cage we now sat. It would be hours before dawn, which meant we were in for another long night.

"You need to tell me everything this time because he didn't do that himself. He doesn't have the power to make an eclipse happen, and he just somehow managed to make the earth bow to him. I need to know what we're facing here, and Clara is stuck in the middle of it with us now." She moved to Clara, sliding down the wall to sit beside her. Clara lifted her eyes to mine as she hiccupped between sobs. I sighed in response and I moved to sit beside them, pulling my knees to my chest as I frowned with the memories that scratched to the surface, peeling the scabs of the wounds he'd left.

"I'm so sorry, Clara. You shouldn't be here," I whispered past my dry tongue. "You too, Laura. I knew he'd come for me eventually, but I figured if we were never out at night, he couldn't get past the runes to reach me or hurt us. I've been very careful never to be outside during the night or close to dusk."

"Why are they doing this to us?" Clara croaked as she leaned her head against my arm, while Laura patted her back. "What did you do to him that made him come for you, Avery? He came in daylight, and that is supposed to be impossible for them to do." She pulled her legs tighter against her chest, lifting her head to stare at me as she wiped at her red, tear-streaked eyes. Her strawberry blonde hair was matted and clung to her face as she hiccupped again.

"That's a long story, Clara," I responded guardedly as I heard the vampire who guarded us shuffle on his feet, listening to us discreetly. I swallowed past the lump in my throat and reached up, pushing her hair away from her face. "It's not a story for young ears, nor one you need to hear. I will do whatever it takes to keep you both alive. You know that. You have nothing to fear, it will be okay."

"You know who he is, don't you? He is the prince, isn't he? The one you slept with? Avery, what did you do to make him wish for war against us? I'm not in this; they didn't come for me. He came for you, and we are caught in the middle of it, so I think we deserve to know what you did, and what he intends to do to us." Clara watched me, absently chewing her lip as she waited for me to speak.

"You're right, you do, you both do," I said as I exhaled and turned to lean my head against the wall of the cell. Laura knew most of the story and had heard it all before, but Clara hadn't heard the details. "I was born before 1665, which is when my story began. I was from one of the most prominent covens of London for that time. Back then, the rules were different. Oh, they were the same where creatures were concerned, but to stray with your enemy meant death instead of banishment by the covenant. I didn't choose to betray my coven or leave them, as many other witches had. I was born into an era of death, and it came for us. During that time, London was besieged by a different type of death. Thousands of people were stricken down with it and died within one week of the first sign of the fever. The Black Death, they called it. Witches were no more immune than mortals, which we didn't know until it was too late. Little was known about the sickness, or how it was spreading so quickly. It took thousands to their graves before people even knew it was among them, or how it spread. My mother, the leader of the coven and most powerful witch of her time, thought to save the humans with our magic. So, together, without knowing our fates, we walked into the sick houses to save those who needed help. By the time we figured out that we weren't immune to it any more than they were, it was too late.

"My mother became feverish on the fifth night; her fingers were covered in black flesh that moved up her hands. I sat with her as, one by one, the others in the coven died around us. I would leave her only to burn the bodies of our sisters; I burned them all, even my mother, as I burned with the fever myself. The healers wore plague masks that looked like the most horrid birds of prey, most wearing the raven to signify death. I can still remember the heat of the fever as it burned my flesh as if I'd been set on fire from within. By the time I fell ill, over sixty thousand people had perished to the sickness that ravaged London and the surrounding cities. It continued to spread quickly, pushing further out into the country. I was alone then, left without a coven or anyone to care for me. I knew I would die, that soon the black poison would cover my fingers and I'd become poisonous to others, so I made my way to the sea to send a warning to the other covens as my mother had asked me to do as she lay dying. I'd intended to reach the piers and send word via the wind that sailed the sea, but the closer I got, the further it seemed. The cool air wafting from the ocean offered relief from the fever that ravaged me. I sat down beside children my age who were dying, and when the men in masks came for them, they took me too. They didn't even burn our bodies. Instead, they threw us into the alley with the trash that littered the street, among piles of the dead to be taken out to the sea and tossed into the waves.

"I lay there for hours, praying for death to come because I couldn't find the strength to get up out of the garbage. Then an angel came, and I thought maybe the Gods had taken mercy on me. I was terrified of dying alone, and worse, I feared him catching the sickness, so I begged him to leave me there in the rubbish among the dead. Conner laughed at me; his eyes were of the bluest skies and purple like the flowers that grew wild in the hills of Scotland, his hair the color of dark wheat fields in full harvest. He picked me out of the pile and promised to save me. He chose to save me, to feed me his precious blood that pushed the sickness away long enough for him to take me to his home. Of course, they were immune to the sickness, since they were the undead.

"His blood didn't fully stop the sickness, though. It

held the inevitable at bay. He struck a deal with a witch named Hemlock Hawthorn, who served his father, the Vampire King of England. It was a mix of two things, a spell and his blood that together made me immortal like him, untouchable by the plague. It worked, but it came with a cost. I have to have his blood once every fifty years, or I become sick, and with it, I would spread the plague to this new world. I didn't stay with him because of the need for his blood, though. I was thirteen years old, an orphan without family or a coven to protect me, but this creature, this man, had saved me. He'd faced down death to keep me safe, and at that age, he might as well have hung the moon and the stars in my name. I was assumed dead, with no one who cared if I lived or died, but *he* did. No inquiries were ever made to see if any of our coven lived through the death. They assumed we had perished, but with good cause. I fell in love with Conner; he wasn't what I'd been told his kind was like, nor did he ever force me to use my magic to benefit him or others. He taught me to wield it with the help of enslaved witches. He never forced me to become his whore or to feed him. Many witches were either a vampire's whore or their personal witch, but Conner wanted neither from me, and I'd have done anything he asked. He wasn't what I thought our enemies were, and every day I lived, I saw it. I saw a man who pulled a dying witch out of the garbage and brought her back to life. At that age, I was old enough to become a whore to his kind, and yet he never allowed it. He was my protector and guard; this creature that had every right to demand I use my powers for him didn't ask it of me. I was old enough to breed, and back then it was expected of girls to do so. On the day I turned sixteen, I went to his bed willingly. I demanded that he make me a woman. He did, and I loved him for it. I never had, nor ever will I love anyone else as I loved him."

"If he loved you, why are we in a cage and you're being accused of killing his father?" she demanded softly, her thin, small frame shaking violently with the chill of the dungeon.

"Because I did kill his father and his entire hive. Conner wasn't created, he was born a vampire to a King and Queen who ruled London and the surrounding hives and nests," I replied hesitantly. "I loved him, but it wasn't enough. I never said he loved me, for I'm not sure that is something they do. He never admitted to it, and I never asked for it. I was his enemy and he mine, which is something we forgot along the way. When he remembered, he left me, and everything changed."

"You killed them because he left you? You should have run or done something else. No wonder we are here, locked up in this cage like animals. He is going to kill us!" Clara cried as her body began rocking with silent sobs.

"It isn't that easy, Clara," Laura chided. "There is a lot more to this story that you don't know, nor will you be told."

"He is going to kill us!" she repeated on a hiss.

"No, he is going to kill me. Maybe I deserve it, maybe I don't. Either way, his blood brought me back to life, and he is the one who can take it from me. He knows that, which is why you are here as collateral and to keep me from bringing them all down as I did their hive in London. You are here to guarantee I behave, which I will. I will do whatever is asked of me to procure your freedom."

"He could kill you, you know that, right? He hates you, and no matter what you once shared, he is after one thing and one thing alone. Revenge," Laura warned.

"I agree with your friend, Avery," Conner laughed wickedly as he stepped from the shadows and stared at me like I was a stranger instead of the lover he'd once cherished above everything else. "Stand up and turn around, orphan. If you whisper a single spell, sweet Clara here will stand in your place for your first night of punishment while you watch."

I did as he'd asked me to and, standing on shaking legs, I turned around and stared at a crack in the prison floor. I could smell the musk from the mold, taste the death that lingered from the last unfortunate soul who displeased the King of the Inland Northwest. These mountains belonged to him now, his territory when he'd come to the Americas. His hands bit into my arms as he clasped them behind my back, locking them into metal cuffs. He pushed me aside as he closed the cell, even as I moved towards Laura's outstretched hand.

"You guys will be okay," I promised through the thickening in my throat.

"But you won't," Laura sobbed as she watched me, swiftly moving to stop me from leaving as if she could pull me back into the cage with them. The moment Conner stepped closer to me, she stopped.

"No, she won't," Conner agreed softly while a dark smile spread over his lips. "She is accused of murder, and will stand trial for her crimes."

I shivered at the hatred that burned in his tone as he

locked the cell, the noise filling the room until he stood behind me. His hands slowly wrapped around me and pulled me against him. The heat of his body filled the chill of my bones as he laughed huskily against my ear.

"Did you miss me while I celebrated your capture, little witch?" he asked.

"That answer is still no. Remember, I never did miss you when you were away. Can we get on with this?" I asked.

"I remember the last time I fucked those pretty lips of yours. I do believe it was right before I left and you slaughtered my entire fucking family, wasn't it?" he purred against my ear, licking it, which sent a shiver racing through me. His fingertips drifted down my arms, sending an electrical hum of his immense power into my core. He turned me around, rubbing his knuckles over my cheek as he studied me. Those piercing, bluish-purple eyes bored right into my soul. Conner reached up, pushing away a strand of midnight hair from my face. His hair was the color of the sand on the beaches when the water drifted over them, cleaning it. His arms were covered in intricate tattoos, some of which I'd given him myself through magic to keep him safe *from* magic, as well as enemies who had sought to end his life prematurely.

"I remember," I uttered hoarsely as desire swept through me. "I also remember you calling me your sweet little plaything, and telling me how I betrayed my people. You told me to run because only death would ever welcome me into its embrace after what we had done together. I would have run, but your father wouldn't allow me to leave, and you knew it. You gave me to them, Conner. If I am their murderer, you handed them to me to slaughter. After all, you brought me back from the dead and said that I was one of you from that point on. So what does that make you?"

"Your personal hell, Avery," he growled angrily as his jaw clenched. "You won't die here, but you also won't ever leave here either. You see, I know how much us feeding bothered you, so what better punishment than to keep you as my blood whore?"

"Why would you want that?" I asked.

"So that I can fuck you whenever I feel like it, and finally taste that sweet blood of yours that I denied myself so long ago. I never did get to taste what I earned. First things first, though, you get to face the others who want your blood as bad as I do." He held out his arm, indicating the dark stairway that led up into the main floors. "Ladies first, or do you prefer Killer of Kings these days? I never did figure out if you took the proper title after everything you've done to us, Avery."

"I prefer Cheveron witch; it makes even other witches uncomfortable when I am in their presence. Speaking of witches, they will come to take me, either to request my death or my release. The covens will never allow me to live long enough to be your whore. That would give their enemies too much power, and not even being King will sway them."

"Mmm, I took that into consideration. I have an entire school full of students from the strongest bloodlines alive as bargaining chips. I think mommies and daddies might argue they want their children back more than one ancient, murderous bitch." I was shoved roughly towards the staircase that led up into the darkened interior of the stone mansion. I tripped on the way up, and instead of preventing my head from crashing against the concrete stairs, he let me fall. Conner could have stopped it easily, but he'd chosen to let me endure the pain. This gentle creature had turned into a monster, and I wasn't sure anything I did or said would change my fate, but if I could change Clara's and Laura's fates, I'd do whatever it took to manage it. There was also the fact that he may have been right: if he held the students, I may not have help coming for us. They meant more than the power that burned through my veins, and I wouldn't fault them for choosing their children over us.

I stayed there for a moment, fighting past the pain as something hot and wet ran down my temple. I could feel Conner behind me, staring at my ass, which was pointed upwards as I fought the nausea and pain that hit me. I realized I was stuck, ass-up and at his mercy.

"Ask me for help, waif," he demanded.

"I'm in no hurry to move from here," I muttered as I felt his palm skimming my ass before it slipped between my legs. I fought the moan that rose from deep in my chest as he rubbed his fingers through my core.

"Get the fuck up, you stink," he hissed as he helped me up. I swallowed down the urge to feel bad about stinking, which was insane since he'd thrown me into the cell so he could celebrate my capture. It was his fault I stunk in the first place.

"Would you like to watch me bathe, Conner?" I asked in a sultry voice that pulled a growl from him. He pushed me against the wall with his forearm against my throat as he stared into my eyes with naked hunger.

"I'll watch you do more than that tonight before

the sun rises, Avery. I have planned this for centuries and have relished the thought of destroying you every fucking night since I returned to discover my father's corpse. You think you can escape me, but I'm buried so fucking deep into the fabric of your being that you can never do so. Your sweet cunt is already weeping at the thought of me destroying it, and I have hardly even touched you. There's also the fact that I'm hungry, and you're looking like my dinner date. I can't wait for you to meet my feeder. I chose her because of you. She endures the pain I wished to give to you, and now that I have you, you will scream for me, orphan. Would you like that? To be fucked like you're nothing to me, like a dirty little cunt that lives to please me? Welcome to hell, imp," he laughed as he pushed me from the darkness into the light of the hall.

CHAPTER THREE

I was shoved to my knees as he took his place on the throne. My clothes were filthy, my hair ratted from the days of endless worrying over Clara and Laura's fates as we were forced to sit in a cell without food or water. His punishment of me I could see, but then he didn't care if I suffered. Clara and Laura, on the other hand, were both innocent. Clara was something pure and light and didn't belong in the darkness where we resided.

The crowd cheered for their King; his prowess of hunting down his prey in broad daylight would be the shit of legends, and even I may have cheered him on if I hadn't been the one caught. I bowed my head, a subtle suggestion of submission, which he noted with a raised brow.

Unlike most of the vampires here, Conner had been born to parents who had royal blood humming through their veins. He was from one of the original lines of born vampires to remain ruling today. Creatures flocked to him in masses since he was one of the strongest vampires in the world. It explained his full hive after I'd destroyed the last one.

"I give you Avery Ilsa Cheveron, the orphan I spared from the Black Death and brought into my home as one of us. My lover, my witch, and my father's murderer," Conner announced as he stared at my bowed head. "How does the hive wish to proceed?" he asked.

"Traitor's death for what she did to our family," Addison's sultry voice filled the room.

"Agreed, traitor's death," another demanded.

"I say you let us all fuck her and feed on her," Royal snapped as he knelt beside me, tilting my chin up to stare into his amber eyes. "I've always wondered what that golden pussy must taste and feel like to have snagged our prince so fully. Or was it magic you used to make my brother blind against your poisonous flesh, slut?"

"What's the matter, Royal? Jealous because I denied you every time you tried to fuck me behind Conner's back?" I asked without lifting my eyes, which was exactly how he landed a blow against the side of my head with his inhuman speed, sending me to the floor and my ears rang as pain rocked through my head.

"I don't believe I said she could be abused, yet, brother," Conner said softly, as if he was reprimanding a child who had asked for his dessert before dinner.

I didn't get up, nor could I with my hands bound behind my back. I stayed there, listening to the heartbeat that raced through my eardrums. Rough hands picked me up and placed me back on my knees at Conner's feet. I refused to meet his stare, even as he asked the room what they thought should be done, and they agreed with his younger brothers and sister, the only family he had left.

"The entire room thinks you should face a traitor's death, little witch," he announced with cold, emotionless eyes that watched me for any sign of weakness. "How do you plead to murdering an entire hive and a King?"

"Plead? I plead nothing. Did I murder your family? Yes," I said, and the room erupted in angry shouts for blood, my eyes lifted to his, holding his angry stare.

"You admit to murdering the King?"

"I boiled him like dirty laundry soaked with the plague, Conner."

His hands tightened on the arms of his throne as he watched me. The muscle in his jaw ticked with his rage as he fought for control over the anger pushing through him with the need to impart violence on me. His chest heaved, his fangs slipping from his gums, and his eyes turned black, soulless.

"So you admit to murdering an entire hive and its King," he growled.

"I do," I agreed.

"You deserve the traitor's death or worse," he uttered thickly.

"No, I do not. I never agreed to serve *your* King. I agreed to be yours, never your whore, never the one you fed on, and never your witch. You placed me within your father's keep, abandoning me to him. I served you and you alone by choice, and in order to deserve a traitor's death, one must first be loyal. I was only loyal to you."

Addison snorted and rose from her chair beside her brother's, swaggering over to me with her war braids on full display as she knelt in front of me. "You belonged to us, you were saved *by* us. That makes you ours."

"No, your brother saved me, and then he freed me. He did so by denouncing his claim to me. He didn't ask, nor did he instruct me that I would become a whore to his father. I never gave you a vow of service, did I, Conner?" I asked pointedly, with unwavering accusation in my eyes.

"I saved your life from the plague, waif," he snapped.

"I never offered you a vow of service, did I, Conner?" I repeated as the memories of being previously subjected to a traitor's death over and over replayed in my mind, from being forced to watch it happening from Conner's lap long ago. "Did you ever ask me to serve you or your father with my loyalty or my solemn vow?"

"No, but then you are alive because of my blood," he growled.

"Under the covenant, I am only to be held to the laws of a race and their punishment *if* I gave a vow of loyalty. My vow to you was to honor and love you. I did both until you told me how unworthy I was of the Prince of the Undead and walked away from me and what I had given you freely. So, if you want my blood, kill me, but I will not stand guilty of treachery when I gave no vow to break."

"You should have left this fucking bitch in the trash to die like the rest of the peasants." Addison's hand twisted in my hair and she lifted me, slamming my face down against her knee as she hissed and brought me back up to my feet, turning to face me. "If we can't kill her outright, I want to fight her."

"My hands are tied behind my back, Addison," I muttered through the pain of my face as my nose dripped blood onto the floor in front of me. "What's the matter, afraid of a fair fight? Or still pissy I took away your daddy, little girl?" I taunted and watched as her fist flew at my face, knocking me back, but not down. I righted myself as blow after blow sent me back until she punched me in the stomach, knocking the wind out of me.

Dropping to my knees, I stayed there a moment before I got back up and watched her eyes turn crimson as she eyed the blood that dripped from my face. She moved faster than my mind or eyes could track her. I was thrown to the ground, and her hot breath skimmed my throat before someone threw her back and stood in front of me.

"No one feeds from her but me, Addison. Not unless I say or permit otherwise. She never promised or offered her loyalty, not even with me pulling her useless body from the garbage, or saving her pathetic life so that she could betray me. She will not face the traitor's death— however," he paused as the room erupted into chaos as I stared up at him. "She will never leave here alive. She will remain as my whore and my feeder until I tire of her and end her life myself."

I coughed, turning to spit up blood as everyone cheered him on like he just announced he was going to take on the world and they were happy about it.

"And when the witches come, what then, Conner?" Mayhem asked, his deep, sultry voice echoing over the cheers and silencing the room. He wouldn't meet my stare, and we both knew why, and yet he was one of the only vampires here who knew the full details of what had happened to me. He chose to protect himself, which kept my secrets from the others.

"Then I inform them that we have over sixty witchlings that were in her care being held at their school, and if they want their children back, she stays to face her charges and full punishment," Conner said nonchalantly as he shrugged.

"And if they demand you release her still? She's the most powerful witch that I know of, and one of the oldest and purest bloodlines. They're not going to settle with her being under your thumb, brother," Addison added, her eyes still crimson as she stared at me.

"Then we will go to war against them, no hive would argue it. She will pay for her crimes one way or another. She isn't leaving here, even if it means war against the witches." Conner stared down at me, his smirk firmly in place as he knelt beside me and pushed the hair away from the blood that was stuck to my face, his finger tracing the curvature of my cheek. "Are you ready to serve me, whore?"

"Free Clara and Laura, or give them water. Clara's young, she won't last if you continue to ignore her needs, and then all the leverage you hold over me is gone. So unless you want to fuck an unmoving corpse, tend to their needs first."

"She was fed and watered the moment you were removed from their cell. You, on the other hand, can fucking beg to be fed and if you're a good girl for me and earn it, I may give it to you."

"You do know that I crave death more than I do sustenance, don't you? Oh, I guess we've been apart awhile. I don't beg to live anymore, because I wish for death. I crave the peace it will offer my soul. I miss my mother and my coven. So, go ahead, threaten me with what I crave most and see what it gets you," I uttered and he shook his head as his eyes darkened with my words.

"If you wanted death, you wouldn't have drunk the blood I sent you. Tell me, did you touch that pretty cunt when you drank it as you used to? Or did you drink it and wish I was with you to destroy that pretty flesh?"

"I was inside a school full of innocent students. Do you think I'm selfish enough to allow the plague to be let loose on innocent lives? I'm fully aware of what happens when I don't drink your blood; how do you think there have been outbreaks of the plague before? So no, I didn't think of you at all, ever."

"Clara and the other bitch stay here to ensure you behave. Until I free them or end your life, you're all at my mercy. If you don't play nice and do what you are told, I'll give that sweet young one to Mayhem to play with, and we all know how sick and deviant he is with an untrained cunt, now don't we?"

"I already agreed to play a good whore for you," I whispered as I struggled to get up, only to fail. I exhaled as I stared up at the vaulted ceiling. "Let's play, Conner. First, you may want to wash me, as I fucking stink."

"You do, and I can't decide if I want to lick you clean and taste your sweet blood or strangle you. So get the fuck up and move. I find myself impatient to hurt you," he chuckled as I once again tried to get up and failed, groaning as more blood leaked from the gash on my forehead and nose. "You're weak," he growled and grabbed my hair, ripping me off the floor as the crowd cheered.

CHAPTER FOUR

I was quickly scrubbed clean and tossed into Conner's room wearing a tiny red nightgown that barely covered anything. My hair had been fashioned into a braid and tied atop my head, leaving my entire neck exposed. The room was decked out in medieval weapons, some I knew he wore when we had been together, while others looked newer, more modern. I moved to the wall, touching the sword I'd bought him one summer after we'd spent most of it in bed together. It shocked me that he'd chosen to keep it, considering everything that had happened.

My eyes strayed to portraits and paintings of a dark-haired girl posed in sinful positions, her face hidden in shadows. The walls were light blue, while the carpet was white and clean. It was an opulent space, one fit for a King, but considering he became King after I murdered everyone who stood in his way of succession, it made sense. It was too bad that he never wanted to be King, considering he had been the kindest, most learned, and best fitted for the position out of the four heirs.

I felt his eyes burning my flesh and ignored him, knowing he was watching me as I looked around his apartment. This was a game we'd often played, him the voyeur and me his victim who had no idea she was being watched. At first, I hadn't known he watched me, and as I grew up, I felt him in the shadows, watching, waiting for me to become the woman I would, and each passing year, he grew more restless for it to happen.

Life was much easier back then, with only the two of us in our bubble. I'd wanted his bite to prove what was between us held so much more than he led on. Eventually, it drove a wedge between us. I'd been much younger than him, and didn't care about the rules that stood between us, or that it was against the covenant. In my mind, we were all that mattered, no one else was in our bed, at least not until he left it and never returned.

I shivered as his hot breath fanned against my neck, he placed a soft kiss against my flesh while I waited for him to speak. He hadn't been hiding where I thought I'd caught movement. His arms wrapped around me and his fangs brushed my flesh.

"Admit that you missed me, little witch."

"Never," I whispered barely loud enough to be heard over the thundering beat of my heart.

His hand wrapped around my throat and he pulled me back against his naked chest. I exhaled, drinking in his sinful scent as I struggled to get air back into my lungs. He was quicksand, my poison, and he'd always known it, exploited it, and I'd loved every moment of it. He was every fantasy I ever had, and even the ones I hadn't. Conner Halverson was my first thought when I woke in the morning and the last before I slept. His presence radiated through the room. He slowly ran his hand down the front of my body, cupping my breast, then slipping it between my legs, pushing aside the laced panties, rubbing his finger through the wetness of my pussy.

"No, you didn't miss me at all, little liar. This cunt is wet for me, isn't it? Does it crave for me to wreck it, to fucking destroy it until it aches for me alone?" he growled and slipped his fingertips through the slickness of my sex, laughing darkly as he pulled away. He stepped in front of me and I struggled to breathe, to regain control of my body while his dark violet eyes watched me. I covered my chest with my hands. He smiled at the effort to shield my body's reaction to him.

His hand reached out, running over the cut on my cheek. Hissing in pain, I moved away from his touch. I was covered in bruises, my face swelling with every passing moment until I feared my eyes would close from the inflammation. He watched me as I brought my hand up to touch my cheek.

"You egged her on," he said, stating the obvious. "You know how Addison is, and your betrayal didn't just hurt me, waif. You hurt us all. We took you in, we kept you alive and safe from the hive, as well as those that would hurt you or wished you harm. You repaid us by killing our brothers and our father," he said harshly, then brought his thumb up to his fang and ripped it open.

I stood in silence, watching as he moved his thumb towards me. Wincing, I recoiled from his touch and the erotic scent of his blood as it filled me with memories from long ago. He laughed at my reaction, and I might have joined him had I not endured the blood that turned me into something else, *someone* else.

"I remember a time when you begged for a taste of me."

"I remember a time when I'd have slit my fucking throat for you. You are not that person, and neither am I anymore," I said as he glared at me, pushing his fingers through the wound roughly before brushing it over my lips while I clamped my mouth closed.

"Open your mouth, little witch."

My lips opened and Conner pushed his bleeding thumb into my mouth. I moaned as my lips clamped around it and sucked it clean. His eyes lowered, watching as he withdrew from my lips. It wasn't enough, but his blood was never enough, not unless it was combined with my own. But it was enough for my injuries, and I felt my wounds healing and closing as my eyes grew heavy with need.

"Why did you do it, Avery?"

"If I told you I did it to survive, would it change how you feel?" I asked softly, my eyes lowering to the floor, unwilling to watch the answer dancing in his glare.

"My father gave his word that you would be released without your memories. You were only meant to remain there until dawn, and then you would have been free of us. I told you to run, and I meant it. You didn't even fucking try, did you? No, instead you took out your anger on those who guarded you. The same people who offered you a home and shelter when you had none."

"Is that what you think they did, guard me against harm?" I asked, my throat tightening as I trembled from the memories.

"It is exactly what they did!"

"How would you know, Conner? You left me. You took Addison, Mayhem, and Royal, and then abandoned me to the mercy of the hive. Do you honestly think after all the centuries I spent in you and your father's care that he ever planned to allow me to walk away from him?"

"Don't talk about my father, waif!"

"Oh, that's right, because he was such a gentle creature? Long may he reign," I hissed and then gasped when his hand connected around my throat, and he pushed me against the wall, my feet hanging uselessly as I kicked them, unable to get air into my lungs. My hands covered his and his forehead rested against mine.

"Do not fucking speak of my father ever again, Avery," he whispered and lifted his eyes to mine. "It's time you learned your new role," he snapped, watching me continue to gasp for air while stars erupted in my vision. "You're no longer mine, which means you're not safe here if I so choose to toss you into the feeder lounge. You took from me, and I will take it out of your flesh. I saved you; I gave you a family and a place to live where you didn't have to look over your shoulder every moment, wondering if you were being hunted, and then you took everything from me. You're a slave, nothing more. Now strip, because it's time I remind you of how little you mean to me, and how easy it was to walk away from you." He released me and watched as I dropped to the ground, hitting my knees on the carpet, sucking air into my burning lungs. His words stung, creating a maelstrom of turbulent emotions that pricked my eyes with tears.

Conner stepped back, turning on his heel as he

moved into the next room. I pushed from the ground on shaky legs, which refused to hold my weight. I sunk back down and placed my head against the wall as tears burned behind my eyes. Conner had never touched me in anger, it was new territory I'd never wanted to wander into, and yet here I was, stuck in it.

"Now! Avery," he said from the doorway.

My head tilted slightly in his direction and I eyed him as I fought the emotions and pain of being at his mercy. I pushed up from the floor, holding onto the wall for support before I stepped toward him. I walked slowly into the bedroom, ducking under the arm he'd placed on the doorjamb.

Inside the room, my gaze wandered over the huge four-poster bed done in crimson sheets with black pillows propped against the headboard. Beside it was a bar, with aged scotch and other spirits he'd probably been around for as they were placed in barrels to age. More pictures of the dark-haired beauty covered his walls, in innocent and sinful poses. I spun around, intending to ask who she was until my eyes settled on the wooden X with chains hooked to the top and bottom. Above it was a picture of the girl posed on the X, her body on display chained to it. The pictures in the apartment weren't of just of any girl, I realized; it was me. In the last one that stood above his bed, my face was revealed. I was in a pose that exposed my cunt, with my lips curled into a smirk, as if the artist had told me a juicy tidbit.

Swallowing hard, I turned, lifting a dark brow in his direction. "You kept the X?" I asked through trembling lips.

"I brought it up from the cellar when I decided it

was time to fetch you. If I recall, you used to enjoy being tied to it as I made you scream."

"I remember. I also remember you accusing me of things I had never done. You also let Royal into the room to threaten me, and at first, I thought your father had sent him. Or, I did. He told me you knew he was there with me, and that soon, you'd share me with the hive. I sobbed and screamed for you, and thought you cared enough to protect me, and then I realized you had let Royal into our bedroom to terrify me. I was an idiot to think that you were some prince in a novel who would defend my honor. Instead, you knew what he did to me, and you allowed it. You wanted me to hate you for it, and I did. You could have released me, allowed me to leave without handing me over to your father; so why didn't you? Hadn't I earned that much from you?"

"You were my enemy," he said, watching me move towards the X. "You couldn't be trusted, and my father needed to know that you wouldn't run to a new coven for shelter and give them everything you knew about us to get back at me for walking away from you. Royal did what he was told to do: scare you into leaving me. You needed a push to leave me, he provided it."

"See, that's the sad reality of this, Conner. I wasn't your enemy then; I was just the stupid little waif who fell for a prince that played with me until he grew bored. I challenged your beliefs, and then I was tossed to the wolves like a piece of meat. Now, here we are, and I am most definitely your enemy," I said, a sad smile playing across my lips as I turned in front of the X to stare back at him.

Reaching down, I pulled the bottom of the nightgown

and lifted it over my head, ignoring him as I hooked my fingers through my panties, pulling them off before standing back up to stare at the floor, eventually finding the courage to lift my eyes. His stare held mine before slowly slipping down to my breasts then further down my frame.

"You haven't changed at all," he whispered harshly, his eyes banking with heat as they lifted again to hold mine.

"Veneer is easy to achieve, but even the ugliest monsters can look pretty with a learned smile, you should know that, Conner. After all, you taught me firsthand, but then you taught me all the hard lessons, except one, didn't you?" I snapped.

"Mmm, I would have to agree. You did murder an entire hive of vampires as they slept, after all," he replied icily, staring at me. "I was wondering when you'd drop the act and show me my little orphan who loved to argue and give me lip. I was beginning to wonder if you had any fight left in you, or if you had become weak hiding in these mountains you thought kept you concealed from me. Imagine my surprise, after centuries of watching you, to discover you were receiving warlocks to breed that pretty pink cunt of yours. How many children did you give them? I bet you found them lacking after knowing me, didn't you?"

"You watched me?" I asked, aghast at the idea after I'd been so careful to remain hidden from him, and yet he'd known I was close to him the entire time. I never went outside after dusk since escaping from his kind, and never before dawn's killing light rose from the east.

"Did you actually think you could hide from me?

I've always known where you were, little witch. From the moment you stepped out of the shadows to board the ship to Salem, I have known your every move, along with every male who entered your hidden little academy in the hills. Did you never wonder why the men who visited you died soon after?"

"You *killed* them?" I whispered, horrified that he'd do something so careless it could have brought a war down upon both races.

"You think I would let them live after they'd slept with my girl?" he chuckled as he stepped closer, boxing me in against the cold wood of the X. "You think you get to walk away from me and live a normal life after everything you did to my people?" he snarled.

"I didn't *sleep* with them," I snapped and watched his mouth curve into a grin. "I didn't; it's true. I didn't allow any of them to use me."

"You expect me to believe that? You have not left this place in over seventy-five years, and when you did leave, even for a brief time, it was to rush across the country to pick up a student and bring them back here. I know, because I followed you."

"You know *nothing*, Conner. I wanted to be here because *I* couldn't be forced to do anything but teach witches how to survive against your kind, which is nothing more than monsters. Men come here to check files, not vaginas! They make sure we have everything we need to teach the children, and to ensure the crystals are charged and the sage is plentiful as well as dried correctly. You killed the clerks," I whispered.

"Sure, let's go with that. Ask me if I fucking care, little witch," he snapped coldly as he folded his arms over his chest and stared at me. "They got what they deserved for touching what belonged to me, the King."

"Should I say that about your father? Those men had families; you want to know what we did when they visited? We looked at pictures of their children who would eventually attend my school because of *their* service to the coven. You murdered innocent men because you were jealous?" I asked as he reached down, captured my hand, and locked it into the cuff above my head. Once he finished securing my other hand, he leaned against my neck, kissing it, then moved lower, flicking my nipple with his tongue before nicking it with his fang. "Don't," I whispered as he licked the path of my blood, tasting it for the first time. He lifted his head, staring at me with blood-red eyes that revealed his hunger. His hands lowered, locking each of the cuffs around my ankles while he continued to lick and taste my flesh.

"You don't get to tell me I can't taste you anymore," he uttered with my blood painting his lips. "If I want to drink you, I will. You murdered my family, and you bitch about me killing strangers? Fuck you, Avery. I told you when I ate your sweet cunt the first time that you would only ever know me in that way, and I fucking meant it."

"You walked away from me, Conner!"

"And I let you go! I walked away because if I hadn't, I'd have fucking done everything I could to keep you, and eventually, we'd have started a fucking war! Is that what you would have wanted? You loved me, but I had a duty to my people that I couldn't walk away from, not even for you. I would have been disowned and hunted down right beside you, Avery. You'd have hated me, you'd have resented leaving the elegant lifestyle I had given you. You would have left me, and what the fuck would I have become?" he stepped back, staring at me as he rubbed his hand down his face, like he couldn't believe we were having this argument two hundred years later.

"Fuck you, waif. You wanted more than I could give you. You tried to destroy me, and bring me down with your pretty pink flesh and your shy smiles. My father knew what you were, he warned me from the moment I brought you home that you should be treated as a slave. He knew you would betray us, and I argued that I could change you. You were sin, placed right in my fucking path like a fucking moth to the flame. I walked right into it, didn't I? I should have heeded his warning that witches are nothing but whores who fuck their way into your world, then take what they want while leaving everything in ruins if you allow them to do so. I didn't want to believe him. Then he showed me how easily you could be turned, and all it took was Royal spending a few hours with you. I tested you, and you failed by spilling our secrets to him. So I agreed it was best you go back to your people. My father promised once I was gone, you'd be free to leave and go back to your people with no memory of us. I fucking wish you had allowed him to do as he planned."

He turned, walking away from me and I watched his stiff back leave the room. The apartment door opened and closed. I blinked, wondering why he'd leave half-naked, but then he was King, and he could do what he wanted. A feminine voice sounded in the room next to me, and I lifted my head, staring at a black-haired female with lime green-eyes.

"Avery," Conner said sharply, walking into the room behind her. "Meet Amery," he laughed, watching as I swung my gaze from her to him. "Amery, meet Avery; isn't she pretty?" he asked.

"Very, can I play with her?" Amery asked.

"No, she's mine to destroy." Conner watched me as he pulled Amery closer, stripping her out of the dress she wore. Her breasts were larger than mine, her stomach covered in bite marks, along with her throat and thighs. "Avery is my prisoner, ignore her, darling. She's nothing. Now bend over, so I can fuck you."

"Look, I don't need to see this," I stated as I watched him moving closer to me.

"Oh, but you will, and if you look away, I will bring in the other prisoners and fuck them both while you watch me destroy their cunts," he growled. "You don't want that to happen, do you?"

"You're an asshole," I whispered.

"You have no idea who or what I am anymore, little witch. You've been away for a long time. You ruined my world, and ran away in the brilliant rays of the sun, hiding for twenty fucking years before I felt you stirring from the shadows to escape from London. I wasn't even sure if you lived, but then I remembered that you couldn't die unless I allowed it. Do you know how much it hurt me to walk into that hall and see everyone dead, Avery? I found my family slaughtered and the evil taint of your fucking magic so thick it made me crave your death. So you don't get to ask to leave this room. You are my prisoner, and you will submit to whatever

I want, or the other witches below will suffer for your unwillingness to cooperate. Tit for tat, let's see how you enjoy it."

"I'm flattered that she looks exactly like me. Really, I am, but it's rather creepy and petty of you. Tell me, my prince, did you name her after me too?" I laughed and I watched him move up behind Amery as she scooted an ottoman in front of me, knowing his game.

"I chose her because she screams when I hurt her, yet still begs me for more. I needed someone who looked like you, so that every time I punish her or she weeps from pain, I can see your face as I imagine it is you I'm hurting. Because every time I slam into her tight cunt, I imagine it's yours and I destroy it."

"Oh," I whispered and swallowed loudly as he walked over to me, watching me tremble for what we both craved, what I would never admit to needing from him. I missed his touch, the feel of his strength when he took control in the bedroom and dominated me for the sliver of time I would allow it. I missed his kisses, his heated gazes that always left me breathless. I watched as he bent down, kissing my cheek before running his fingers through the wetness at the junction of my apex.

"You always did enjoy watching me fuck, didn't you? Naughty little thing that you are, you first thought I never noticed you behind the curtains, touching your innocent cunt as I fucked the whores. I knew you watched me, and your scent drove me to fuck them harder. Let's see if that's still the case, shall we?" he asked as he stepped away from me, leaving me shivering with need.

CHAPTER
FIVE

Amery was positioned before me on all fours, naked on a square-shaped ottoman that barely held her upright as she posed for Conner. Her mouth was mere inches from my exposed nakedness, and yet she didn't make a move to touch me, thankfully. Her eyes watched me with a burning curiosity in their green depths that both terrified and excited me. She wanted to taste me, but worse, she wanted me gone from this room so that she alone could have Conner. There was madness in her lime-green depths as she gazed upon my flesh.

She raised her ass, not needing to be told he was behind her, ready to take what he so readily offered her. The smell of her arousal filled the room as my senses sought to numb my reaction to what was unfolding before me. I knew why he wanted this: so my anger would spike, my sense of need for him would arise, and I'd stake claim to what was mine. More so, he wanted me to know that he'd moved on from me. He was no longer the same creature who had, more often than not, rushed home to fuck me after he'd been off on some duty to his father. He hadn't taken anyone since the day he made me into a woman, not until everything between us had changed.

I watched as he settled behind her, his stare never moving from mine while he pushed his thick cock into her clenching cunt. She cried out as he inched forward, her scream feeding his ego while she watched me, wildness burning in her green eyes. He surged forward, and she moaned as he filled her dripping pussy, and mine clenched with the need to be fucked by him. My legs trembled and I struggled not to look away as she screamed out his name while he slowly, methodically, moved behind her.

My eyes dipped to where they were connected and anger rushed through me, ripping my magic to the forefront as pain rocked through me. My moan wasn't of pleasure but filled with pain as the runes inside the room glowed with warning while magic seeped from my pores, seeking out her heart to crush it where it beat quickly for him.

"Tsk-tsk, no magic, waif," he said huskily, enjoying the pain that ripped through me. "If you try to cast in this room, it will only hurt you. Be a good a little bitch and watch me fuck Amery's tight cunt," he crooned as he began to move behind her.

The sound of flesh meeting flesh filled the room. The scent of Amery's cunt flooding with heady arousal fed my own need, forcing my pussy to weep with the demand to be filled. It didn't go unnoticed as I clenched for him. I could feel the arousal of my sex leaking down my leg, creating a slick mess for him to easily fill me, and yet I didn't want it or him. I wanted to escape this room, escape what was happening before me and hide my shame in the darkness of night that filled the world beyond these walls.

Conner's fangs filled his mouth as I watched, and that only added to the arousal that pooling between my thighs. A moan bubbled up to escape past my lips as heat unfurled in my belly, building with frustration from being neglected while I watched him take her over the edge with his thick, massive cock that he continued to bury into her welcoming flesh. My body trembled violently at the memories of fangs tearing into my flesh, and no matter how much I tried to stop them, tears filled my eyes and rolled down my cheeks as I fought the nightmarish memories of how they felt buried in my flesh.

Conner's eyes seemed to zero in on my salty tears and then lowered to the arousal dripping down my legs for him. There was no denying I wanted him, that I wanted Conner to rid himself of Amery and use me instead. The fact that my tears fell unchecked seemed to confound him, and yet he didn't slow his body as she bucked and begged him for more. I shook harder as he gripped her head, pulling her throat closer to the deadly fangs that would drain her life essence the moment he broke through her flesh.

I wanted to feel those fangs when I'd been younger, naïve against what he truly was. I'd wanted to experience his immortal kiss more than I wanted to draw air into my lungs, and yet now that I knew how much they hurt, and how much pain they could inflict, I no longer craved them.

Conner wasn't even aware Amery was screaming his name, or that her body was trembling around his from shock. It was as if she wasn't even in the room as we watched each other. He didn't want her; he wanted me. Conner used her because he'd craved me as surely as I still craved him. I'd watched him with lovers before, when he pretended not to know I was there, watching him with my clumsy fingers touching my virginal cunt as I imagined I was his lover instead of whatever feeder he'd been using that night. We'd played cat and mouse for years until I'd finally aged past an adolescent teenager into a woman. I knew he suspected I was there, just as I'd known every time he'd stood in the shadows, watching me come undone as I'd bathed alone. It was as if gravity had been pulling us together until it had ripped us apart. I'd craved his fangs, needing to know why the feeders screamed and came undone the moment they sank into their flesh. We'd been on a collision course, one we both had wanted to happen. He'd given me time to blossom into a woman, and I'd begged him to make me one, but soon after, everything had turned dark.

My breathing hitched as the scent of their bodies fucking continued to fill the room. My mind replaced Amery with me, and my entire body heated with an embarrassing need. I felt my sex flexing, aching to be filled by him. I watched those white, pristine fangs push into her throat while she bucked and screamed as the pleasure became too much. He'd never fed from me, ever. I was off-limits to him, or had been when we were lovers. He had never been anything but gentle with the child I'd been, never rough with me as I knew he wished to be, craved to be. I was his waif, an orphan with no one who wanted or loved her, so he had given me what I needed, until the day he'd walked away without a second thought.

Violet-blue eyes lowered to my clenching, dripping wet cunt, and smiled around the mouthful of Amery as he found me drenched and aching for him. I wanted to tear my eyes from what he was doing, and yet I knew he wouldn't make idle threats, he never had. It was one of the things I had loved about him. This was his world, a part that I had never been forced to watch until I'd been thrown into center stage, and now he was punishing me for betraying him.

Her screams filled the room, the coppery scent of blood a perfume that drove the monster to push her boundaries, fucking her without care. The sound of their bodies meeting in pleasure made my heart ache, but watching him with her turned me on, and I hated that part the most, because no matter what had happened, or would, I wanted this monstrous bastard to use me instead of Amery.

Conner pulled away from her vein, letting her uncoagulated blood run down her full, round breast as he smiled up at me, his monster unleashed and she whimpered as he bucked harder, without mercy, into her tight cunt.

"You're wet, waif," he growled huskily, uncaring of the body he fucked as his eyes took in my state of arousal.

"My King, please help me," she whispered as he gripped her hair, and pushed her face to the bench. "I'll bleed out." Neither of us paid her any attention as the heat between us took precedence in the room.

"Close her wounds, Conner. She isn't whom you want to destroy; I am," I whispered thickly through the emotion that tightened my throat. "She'll die, and dying humans are messy. Be a gentleman and tend to your dinner, and stop pretending it's my cunt you're fucking."

He laughed darkly and gripped her by the hair roughly, pulling her to his mouth as he used his tongue to close her wounds. Conner's eyes never broke their stare as they watched me. He pushed Amery away from him and he strode towards me.

"My King?" she whimpered from the floor where he left her.

"Get the fuck out, Amery. Now," he ordered as he stood before me, his chest rising and falling while we silently stared at one another. She rushed from the room, leaving only her scent behind as he stepped even closer, intending to fuck me.

"No," I uttered as his lips brushed over my throat. "Not like this, Conner."

"I'm going to fuck you, Avery," he snarled as his fingers found my sex, pushing through the slickness he'd created with his whore. "You want me to fuck you."

"I do, but not like this. Not with her arousal still covering your cock. If you want me, you will wash her from your flesh and take me after you've cleaned her from it."

"You don't get a fucking choice here. You don't get to tell me what I will or will not do to you anymore. You're my fucking prisoner, so if I want to fuck you with the scent of her pussy still covering my cock, I will."

"If you do this, you will have to rape me, for I will not allow it. You want me willing; I know you do. You want me to submit to your will, to your desire, and I want that too, Conner. I want to fuck you. I want to ride that cock until you beg me to stop, until you turn me over and take me to the edge of the abyss with you. I won't do that with her scent coating your flesh."

"You don't know what I want anymore, waif. You don't know whom I have become, and I don't really fucking care if you want it or not. You killed any kindness I held inside of me when you murdered everyone I loved. Do you think it really matters to me if you submit or not? I don't plan to be gentle or easy with you anymore. I'm going to fuck you like the dirty little whore you are." His mouth crushed against mine and I refused to kiss him back. I refused to taste her blood still coating his lips, and it irked him that he found me unwilling to concede to his dominance or power.

"Don't fucking kiss me with her blood still painted upon those lips of yours," I snapped, staring him down in open challenge. "You don't get me until you've washed her from your mouth and cock, Conner. You need me to submit, that part of you has not changed."

"I don't fucking care if you submit. You want me, this tight pussy is soaking wet for me and me alone. You will take what I give you!"

"I will *not!*" I shouted back at him as he smiled coldly and moved his mouth to my throat. "Conner, no," I whimpered as I felt the scrape of his fangs at the soft column of my throat. "Not like this. Not with her blood taking away from mine. Do you want her taste corrupting mine when you've waited so long to taste me?" I whispered huskily, my eyes dropping with the heaviness of my arousal and need. He'd never taken my blood, and he'd wanted it so fucking badly, yet he'd respected my boundaries.

"I won't be denied anymore, Avery. I will taste every inch of you and know what your blood tastes like before this night is over."

"Fine," I whispered and swallowed harshly. "Just don't do it like this. I wanted you to know my taste and mine alone. I don't want it corrupted by hers. Let me bathe for you, and wash her from you, Con, let me give you what you crave freely without anything else corrupting it. Give me this, and I will give you all of me."

"You think I care about what you want or need anymore?" he chuckled darkly as he lifted blood-red eyes to hold mine.

"I think you do," I uttered huskily. "I think you want to hurt me, and I want you to. I think you want me to submit, and I will. I want this, I do. I just don't want you to do it like this. I want you buried so fucking deep inside of me that I no longer know where I end and you begin, but not with her coating that magnificent cock. I want to taste me on your cock when I fuck it with my mouth. I want to feel it destroying me without her between us."

"Is that what you want?" he asked, stepping back and taking in the dripping state of my flesh as it wept to be fucked by him.

"Yes," I whispered as his eyes burned every inch of my flesh they gazed upon.

"You enjoyed watching me fuck Amery, didn't

you?" he asked, and I swallowed hard past the lump that formed in my throat. "This pussy is dripping with the need to be fucked, isn't it?" His hand moved closer, and the tips of his fingers slid through the wetness of my flesh before he brought them up, sucking each one clean of my arousal as I watched him.

"I'm a woman, Conner. My body responds whether I want it to or not. Watching you fuck a feeder has always been erotic, but that doesn't mean I want to be fucked by you. It never did, but watching you fuck someone has always made my body respond. Don't twist it into something else. I get off watching others fuck too; it's a natural reaction to a basic instinct ingrained in the very fiber of our being. Don't assume I'm that scared little girl who watched you from the shadows, wondering what it would feel like to be the one you used; to feel the sting of your fangs as they punctured her flesh. I'm not her anymore. I'm not the little girl who thought you hung the moon and stars in her name. I learned my worth and what I meant to you. I don't fantasize about being your mate, or thinking I am anything other than what I am: your disposable enemy," I said as I watched him bend down to free one foot and then the other.

His tawny head was bent down as he released my legs, and I closed my eyes. I relished his touch, but the moment he freed my legs, he slammed his mouth over my wetness, slurping it loudly as he fucked me with his mouth until I was teetering on the edge of no return, about to be shot into the stars with a forced release. But he stopped short of it happening, pulling his sinful mouth away from my cunt.

"You taste like heaven, but then you always did.

Avery, you are my prisoner, and from this point on, you will do as I tell you to, or I will bring your friends into this room and chain them to my bed and make you watch as I fuck and drain them. If that is what it takes to make you bend to my will, I won't hesitate to use them."

"You won't like what happens if you do that," I warned harshly.

"You're not hearing me, waif. I don't give two fucking shits what you want or don't want anymore. I want to hurt you; to make you feel what I felt when I walked into my father's home and found everyone dead. You took from me, and you will appease me, or I will begin to destroy everything you care about slowly to be sure you feel what I did."

"I hear you. I also know you, Conner. You want me to give you what you crave. You want me at your mercy, and so I am. You want me to give you what you want, but you can't do that by force, and we both know it."

"I can make you do whatever the fuck I want you to do, imp."

"You could make me do anything you wanted me to, that much is true. You don't work like that, though, my prince. You want me to kiss you because I crave you as much as you crave me. You never took what wasn't freely given. You need pretty things to need you, to feel you so deeply within them that they offer themselves to you because it is the only thing they will ever need. You never forced me to do anything, nor will you. You're a monster who wants the innocent creatures of the world to crave your depravity and offer their throat to your beast. I am not the scared, damaged, abandoned child that I was when you first found me. Back then, I was alone. So alone that when you wrapped your arms around me and promised me you would always protect me, I honestly believed it. I offered you my throat and my cunt. I gave you everything that I could, of my own will, and you relished it. You never took my blood, because you and I both knew we could be something deeper if we did. We are forbidden, though, and maybe that was why you craved me so much. Hell, maybe it was why I wanted to be yours more than I wanted air to fill my lungs. We were on a collision course, and neither of us cared about the consequences, not until you walked away. I'd have been your whore if you had asked it of me, and I think you knew it. That was then, and this is now. I'm not your girl, not anymore. I'm not alone. I found a purpose that was more than sitting at your feet, waiting for your touch. Make no mistake, Conner. I am not here because I want to be. I am here to face charges for what I did, and nothing else. I'd murder them again if I could. So if you need to force me, feel free to do so, because when I walk out of here, and I *will* walk out of here, it will be with my head held high and you behind me, again."

"I am going to get your bath started, and you will wash your body and ready it for me. I don't give a shit if we are forbidden anymore. Nothing can change what you did to my people. You mean nothing to me. You are here as my prisoner, not my guest. If I wish to fuck your cunt, I will fuck your cunt. If I wish to drain you dry, I will. You are nothing. I told you when I left you with my father that you were a fun challenge to who I was, but we were finished. You were my enemy, one who fought me and then caved to my seduction, and when

I'd had my fill of you, I left you where you belonged. You could have walked away from me and not become my enemy. You should have allowed my father to clear your memories and erase us from your mind so you could have walked away free instead of being hunted by me. Now, now you will never walk away from me. You will remain here as my personal feeder and whore. You start your position tonight, Avery. Let's see how you enjoy it, shall we?"

CHAPTER
SIX

I stared at the opulent quartz clawfoot tub that even now was being filled with bucket after bucket of warm water. Conner stood before it as the small children added more water. His hands worked the flowers, pulling the petals from the peonies as he added oil, petals, and smelling salts to the bath. I'd once craved this part of our relationship.

To him, a woman was never as vulnerable and exposed as she was during her bath. It left them at the mercy of whoever happened upon them. I'd often bathed for him, even though he hadn't been aware I'd felt his presence during that time. I'd known he watched me from the shadows of my room, a silent predator that took in every curve of my untried body. My throat exposed from my hair being pinned to the top of my head as I invited the monster that lurked to feast upon what I so freely offered him, and yet he never had.

He pushed his wet, freshly showered hair away from his face as he lifted his head, turning to stare at me where I had slid down the wall beside the X and stayed as the water was filled to the rim of the tub. Conner had the tub created for me. He'd hired an artist to build it from the rare crystal quartz of our time. It replenished my magic, fueling my fire and arousal, which he enjoyed even though, back then, I'd been an innocent creature. I had remained pure until the day I'd turned sixteen, when my body became more woman than child.

It had been the turning point in our relationship. I'd slipped into that tub, touching and playing with myself as he watched me. I'd driven him to the edge of sanity as he'd hidden in the shadows, and the moment he thought to slip away unnoticed to find a feeder, I'd come with his name on my tongue, and he turned my fantasy into a new reality.

Conner made me a woman, and I'd begged him to. I'd spent every waking moment in his arms or riding him until neither of us could move. Weeks turned into months, and months into years where neither of us sought relief in another's arms. Feeders who craved him hated me, becoming the prince's food source and nothing else, because I gave him everything he wanted, everything he craved. I continued doing so until I told him that I loved him and that I wanted to create a life with him, one that we could raise together. And for a while, we both seemed to want it and felt the pull to do just that together. He changed soon after that; with me in his arms and his cock buried deep in my warmth. He turned cold because of his father and his words against me, as if ice water had been doused over his head. Within a month, he'd abandoned me to the mercy of the hive, which held no love for me or what I was. Their sworn enemy now left to them and at their mercy.

"That's enough water," he said, pulling me from my memories, I stood, uncaring that the kids watched me as I moved to stand beside Conner's naked form. "Bathe," he demanded, and I nodded, slipping into the heated tub, ignoring the bite of the water as it seared my flesh, turning it pink.

I brought my knees up to my chest and released my hair to slide down my back, into the water. I reached for the soap, letting my ass lift from the water as he watched me from the shadows of the room. I had just grasped the soap when I felt the power in the room sizzle with his overwhelming presence. Ignoring him, and sitting back, I dropped my legs open and began to clean the junction of my sex, knowing his eyes took in every minute move my hand made as I washed my sex and the inside of my thighs. My hands moved, imagining it was his hands instead of mine caressing me. It was what he wanted, for me to forget who caressed me, forget who watched me as I cleaned my flesh to prepare for his touch, for his mouth to follow the trail of soap.

"Lower, imp," he ordered as my hands stilled. I lifted my head, watching as obsidian eyes locked with mine, and then nodded to my hands. I dropped the soap, forgetting it as my hands touched and skimmed my flesh where I needed him to replace mine. My breathing grew labored as my fingers slid through the soft folds, pushing into my pussy. I lifted my hips and a soft moan exploded from my mouth as I arched into my touch. "That's a good girl," he urged as he climbed into the tub and lifted me, pulling my arms over his shoulders as he brought my mouth to his. "How many men have tasted what belongs to me?"

"Many," I replied honestly.

"How many men have you slept with?" he repeated the question differently.

"Are you asking how many men have fucked me? Many have taken what *you* abandoned. Many have tasted my throat and my cunt, and *many* have fucked and taken what once belonged to only you." I stared into his eyes while he glared at me as if I had somehow betrayed him when it was the other way around.

"You once promised me no other man would ever touch what belonged to me," he uttered hoarsely as his thick cock rubbed against my belly.

"I also loved you once, which isn't the case anymore," I whispered, staring down at his naked chest, where my name had been written beneath his ribs. It was held in the place for those who had died or been taken too soon, which neither was true. I chewed my lip and he studied me staring at my name upon his flesh as he held me in place on his lap with my hands braced on his shoulders.

"When was the last time you took a lover?"

"Two hundred years ago," I replied as he leaned over, kissing the wildly beating pulse at the base of my throat.

"Liar, I have seen the warlocks that come and leave your school. I have murdered them to learn more about the woman you have become. I know they were sent to breed you, just as I know they all died for even thinking about your tight pussy. I'll ask you once more: when was the last time this cunt was filled by a man?"

"Two hundred years ago was the last time I allowed a man to fuck any part of me," I repeated and then flinched as a deep growl rose from his chest. "You killed men who I never allowed to fuck me, just because you were jealous at the mere thought I may have taken a lover?" I uttered barely above a whisper as everything inside of me craved his touch. "You left me, so I'm not sure why it would bother you if I took lovers. It would also be none of your damn business if I did, Conner."

"Know this, little witch: No one will ever breed you unless it is me. You are mine and mine alone. I gave you life when no one else cared if you lived or died. I pulled you from the garbage and brought you back from death. No other man will ever know the pleasure of your body and live to tell about it. I warned you of that when I fucked you the first time. You are mine alone, until the day the true death comes for us."

"I don't see why you would care who fucked me. You abandoned me to a fate worse than death. You gave me to an entire hive of men who wanted me dead. I didn't break my vow to you; you broke yours to me. You abandoned me, and I did what I had to do to survive."

"I want you to tell me what happened when I left you."

"You left and handed me to my enemies to be done with as they pleased, and so they did."

"My father adored you, he doted on you, and you murdered him. I want to know why you turned against us, or were you placed in that pile of bodies to lure me in from the beginning? You see, I've been running it through my head since the day I returned to find the entire hive slaughtered, and none of it makes any sense. You loved us, or I thought you did. Now, I'm not so sure. I'm starting to think word got out that I enjoyed fucking and playing with witches, and they dropped the perfect little dark-haired, green-eyed witch into my path. I think you were planted because they knew I'd save you. I think you earned your way into my hive on your back beneath me, and when I thought you could be trusted, you were given free rein of the hive. I don't think you murdered the hive alone; I think someone helped you and I want to know who it was. So which is it? Were you planted and everything we shared a farce, or did you turn against us because I left you and your fucking pride was hurt?"

"I did it to survive," I whispered as I held his gaze. "I didn't hate you for leaving me, not until later. I fought to survive," I uttered, and before I knew what he'd intended, I was shoved beneath the water and I scratched his arms trying to hold on, to escape the watery grave he held me beneath. My nails scraped over his flesh as I sucked water into my lungs. He lifted me, holding me up by my hair and he shook me.

"That's a fucking lie! You were to be spoken to, your mind erased, and then freed to find a coven that would accept you for what and who you were. You destroyed the hive. Why, because I left you to keep you safe? You wanted to create a child who would have been unnatural, and my father forbid it, and made sure I did what I had to do to protect you. Both of our races would have sought our deaths for creating such a thing, and you were too blind and stupid to realize it. You wanted to be my wife, and you were beneath me. My father made me see what you were, and how wrong what we shared was, and thank fucking God he did, or we'd have been hunted down and burned alive! You spelled me, and I was unable to stop fucking you. You used your magic against me, it was the only thing that made sense, and he had Hawthorn undo the spell you used on me."

"Your father never loved me! He hated me. He hated that you wanted me, that you craved me! He never cared if I lived or died, or if I walked out of that hive alive! I never used magic against you, ever!"

"Shut your fucking mouth!" he demanded as he grabbed my hair, pulling me out of the bathtub with him as he shoved me, sending me slipping across the tiled floor. I went down hard, but wouldn't stay down.

I whimpered as I stood up, waiting for him to offer me a towel, or anything to dry myself with, and yet it never came. Instead, his hands gripped my hair and he swung me around, crowding my space as he walked me back until my ass touched the wall. He pushed me down and reached with his other hand to capture mine, shoving them against the wall as he released my hair in a quick, calculated move. My eyes lifted to his and he watched me, not speaking or moving as anger radiated off of him in waves.

"Open your mouth," he demanded huskily, and I did, pushing my tongue out as I watched his eyes turn obsidian, filling with stars of blue and purple as his true eye color tried to peek through the darkness of his anger. He used his hand to guide his cock into my mouth, and then lunged, sending it deep into my throat without warning. Water filled my eyes as I swallowed again and again to accommodate him. "Good girl," he groaned as he moved his hips, pushing in more as tears rolled down my cheeks from the burning pain as he stretched my jaw. He continued moving, pushing his massive cock deeper as I swallowed and gagged around him, unused to taking anything in my throat. I took him all and watched as he stared down at me, using me as he needed until he pulled away violently, releasing my mouth and my hands all at once. I leaned forward, gagging from the sudden withdrawal. He knelt and grabbed me by the throat as he pulled me up with him.

My hand lifted, intending to slap the smug smile from his face, but he easily deflected it. Conner pulled my hair roughly, and growled as he lifted my struggling form and carried me to the bed. There, he secured my hands to the canopy of the bed, high above my head, forcing me to rise on my knees to balance. Conner walked around the bed, pulling my legs apart as he took in my exposed position. I watched him as he walked back around to where I stared, positioned awkwardly and unable to do anything other than watch him. His hands moved forward, cupping my small breasts as he leaned close to my ear. "You want it rough, imp, I can give you it rough. I can make you know pleasure with your pain, and make you beg me for fucking mercy. I'll bite, let's play, little imp." He laughed darkly and stepped away, leaving me to sit upright with my hands high above my head.

"You want to play rough? Let's play rough, Avery," he chuckled darkly, walking behind me. I felt the bed moving, weighed down by him as he knelt between my legs and let his finger trace over my inner thigh. I watched the thin line of blood as it slid from my flesh. I turned, staring back at him and he smiled. "Mmm, you look good helpless," he growled as his fangs continued to grow in his mouth. His finger pushed into my clenching sex from behind, then another entered me as he drove them into my body until my cunt clenched around them hungrily. He withdrew, walking around the bed to stare at my helpless position before he knelt in front of the bed, staring at the thin slice at my thigh. He ignored it, moving towards my cunt, and his tongue slipped through my dripping flesh before he pulled away, cleaning both the mess and blood that covered my thigh.

"Conner," I cried as he watched me from where he licked the cut clean and then slid his tongue through the mess again. He pushed his fingers into my body, and I cried out as he used them to fuck me. His fingers were relentless as he drove them in and out of my body, gauging my need from the violent tempest my heartbeat became as it raced. The moment I was about to fall over the cliff, he withdrew, moving around the bed to pull my legs back until I gasped as my arms burned from stretching in the restraints. It left my mouth lowered, and I watched as he walked back around, his strides sure as he reached down, stroking my chin while he watched me moaning against the pain. His eyes burned with liquid fire, obsidian with sparks igniting them. He used his other hand to stroke his cock while my eyes lowered to watch. He grinned, knowing the moment realization entered my mind.

"Open that dirty lying mouth of yours, imp," he demanded, and when I opened it to protest, he pushed his cock deep into my throat. I moaned around the fullness of it as he buried himself to the hilt and plugged my nose. My arms burned, my throat ached with the fullness he created, and all the while his other hand worked my throat, forcing me to swallow again and again as he stared at me. I was suffocating on his cock, and he knew it. Lights burst in my vision, dancing in it as consciousness seemed to diminish. I stopped fighting it, knowing that if he chose, I wouldn't make it out of here. My immortality wasn't like his; I could be killed by him and only him if he chose to do so. "Suck my cock, Avery," he demanded, and I blinked as I shook my head.

"Ung," I moaned as I shook my head again and then gasped when he pulled out, moving around me to settle on the bed. "Conner," I muttered hoarsely as I felt him moving behind me. I lifted my ass, needing him to fuck me, and yet he didn't do as I wanted him to.

Instead, he rubbed his cock against my opening, teasing me until I whimpered and begged as his dark laughter filled my ears. His hand snaked into my hair, pulling it back as he lifted my head, turning my neck, kissing the wild, hammering pulse before his fangs sank into my carotid artery as his cock ripped past the layers of scar tissue when he entered my clenching cunt. I screamed as the hardest orgasm of my long life ripped me apart until all I could do was feel him as he destroyed me. He'd not stopped at the scar tissue from the torture I'd endured or noticed that I hadn't actually been fucked in over two hundred years, and shit had grown back. Things like a hymen, which the coven medics said had layers of thick scar tissue from the trauma I'd survived.

My pussy ached, and the sound of him feeding on me filled the room, colliding with the sound of sex as body hit against body while he fucking destroyed me. I felt him pulling back as his tongue closed the wound to my throat, and then he cussed in a violent volley of echoing choruses that I was beyond hearing. My hands were released from the chains, and I turned, pushing him down and taking control, forcing him into my tightness as pain and burning ripped through me.

I stared down into his violet-blue eyes as tears slid from my cheeks to land on his chest. His hands lifted, cupping my breasts, but I pushed them away, ignoring the phantom pain that ached more than my clenching, dripping cunt as I raised on my feet, sliding down him over and over again until the next orgasm took me beyond the pain, past the pleasure, and straight to euphoria. I screamed his name over and over again and he flipped me onto my stomach and lifted my legs apart, entering me hard and fast until I was bucking against him with wild abandon as he sent me reeling into the next orgasm and then the next, which followed violently behind the other.

I felt him tense behind me, pulling me up as he remained buried inside my warmth. His fangs pushed through my throat, and I moaned, muttering incoherently as he drank deeply from my vein until the room swam in my vision. He continued to lift my hips, slamming me down onto his thickness until I went limp in his hold.

I felt his tongue closing the wounds as he held me tightly, never withdrawing from my body as he brought us down onto the soft mattress, pulling me tightly against him as the room continued to spin around me. He never spoke, not until I shivered as the ache he'd created in my body released and blood pooled between my legs, slowly covering the sheets.

"Jesus, Avery," he uttered as he sat up, looking at the

bed where it was covered in blood. "What the fuck?" he demanded, but I had no words. My mouth refused to open, as my eyes grew heavy and closed. I could feel the blood escaping my body, a never-ending river that oozed past the tears and scar tissue inside of me. "Don't go to sleep, little witch," he demanded as he grabbed my face between his palms.

"Fuck you," I moaned and pulled my face from his hold, closing my eyes.

"Why the fuck is there so much blood?" he demanded. "Drink," he instructed. Too tired to argue it, I drank the blood that dripped into my mouth, knowing that once I did, we'd be at this again. In my system, he was an aphrodisiac in which I couldn't get enough. He and I both knew where it led, and while it terrified me, he would take full advantage. I lifted my head, kissing his hand as he watched me, heavy eyes filled with lust as he shook his head. "You're still as beautiful as the day I took you and made you mine. You are mine now, from this day until your last. I will slaughter any who think to take you from me."

"I'm not yours; you walked away from me. You lost me, and you don't get to have me back. I would have walked through fire at your side, or done anything you asked me to, but the moment you left me, you lost me."

CHAPTER SEVEN

I awoke to the sensation of something rubbing against my cheek. Turning my face, I stared into turbulent violet eyes that watched me, studying my reaction as the events from the night before came rushing to the front of my mind. I'd screamed his name, begged him for more, and worse, I'd enjoyed every minute of it, even the overwhelming pain of him tearing through the scar tissue.

"You made quite the mess, imp," he said with a huskily seductive tone as he watched me carefully.

I continued to stare absently at him, wondering what game he played now. He wanted to hurt me, but he didn't act like that was his purpose. He seemed keen on keeping me, on using me as he needed or wanted. Conner wanted to know the past. He didn't want to hear the truth; he wanted to punish me, to get revenge for what I'd done. I pulled my cheek away from his thumb and turned to face away from him, knowing he wouldn't allow it.

The moment I'd turned from his stormy gaze, he

pulled me close against the heat of his body. His fingers trailed over my hip, dancing over my flesh, sending chills racing down my body. Lips pressed against my neck, and the sensitive flesh where he'd bitten me ached and burned for more. His bite hadn't been like the others, his had sent pleasure racing through me so white-hot that I'd unraveled for him, coming undone from the multitude of sensations it had created through my entire system.

"You were a virgin again, how is that even fucking possible," he said as his tongue rubbed over the twin puncture marks he'd left on my throat as a claiming mark to others. When I didn't respond, he rolled me onto his long frame, lifting his hips as his cock hardened beneath my soft folds. His hand touched the amulet that was cradled between my breasts before his eyes left it to stare into mine. "What is this?"

"I told you, I have not been fucked in over two hundred years, and shit grows back. Not to mention, it was well used by others, and the sort of shit that happened to it, well, it had some internal scarring. Rough sex is what the coven medic called it, I believe." I stared at him as he watched me, dropping his gaze back to my amulet as if he was done speaking of the men I'd allowed to fuck me. "It's an amulet, Conner," I replied, watching him closely as he studied it.

"What is it for?" he pressed.

"Don't ask me that," I uttered and tried to move from him as dark memories swept through me.

"It's spelled," he growled. "It's also powerful. Take it off," he demanded as he reached for it. I grabbed his hand, moving it down my body as I lifted to stare down at him.

"It is very powerful, and it is also spelled to never be removed from my throat. If you try or have your witch try to do so, you and he will die," I uttered as I slid over his rigid length that teased my naked flesh. "When will you release Laura and Clara?"

"When you fully submit to me and agree to my terms," he countered.

"I did submit to you," I replied carefully as I stared down to where my flesh was swollen from his cock and touch, lifting a brow at him. "Have I not pleased you? And what terms, I thought I am to be your whore and feed you, is that not enough punishment?"

"You fucked me, but you did not submit. As for the terms, I have not decided what they will be yet. You murdered a King, and punishment for that is death, and yet after all this time, I can't bring myself to murder you. I've considered a few things I want to do to you."

"And that would be?" I asked, uncertain I wanted to know what he'd considered for me.

"You will remain here as my feeder, that much is a given. You will give me the use of your body to do as I wish. That means anything I want, I can do to you, and you will allow it and welcome it. If I want to fuck your throat, I will, if I want to penetrate your perky ass, I will. The hive expects punishment for the crimes you committed though, and so do I. I've considered having you give back what you took from me."

"Give you back what exactly?" I asked carefully.

"My family. It is no longer forbidden for us to create life, and you took my family from me. It seems only fair you give me one back."

I stared down at him as nausea churned in my belly. "You want me to give you children?" I asked, making sure I hadn't misunderstood his words.

"Yes," he chuckled darkly. He lifted my hips and pushed into my body, and I moaned as he filled me full, stretching me wide. "You will give back the family you stole from me, orphan."

"I can't," I uttered hoarsely as he lifted my hips and my sex cradled the head of his thick cock. He slammed me down hard, my head rolling on my shoulders as the moan escaped past my lips and I took what he gave, rocking my hips for more.

"You can and you will," he growled as he rolled us and, towering over me, he stared into my eyes. "I've tasted you, imp," he hissed. "I know you are mine, and I won't ever let you go now. I feel you, Avery. I have felt you inside of me since the moment I pulled your scrawny ass out of the pile of bodies in that dark alleyway beside the pier. I knew tasting you would ruin me, so I never did, but now that I have, you are mine. You won't leave here, ever."

"I will," I argued as he slowly rocked his hips. "I will either leave here on my own, or you will bury me. I am too much of a threat for the coven to permit me to remain here with you. I hold too many of their secrets to allow an enemy to control me. We both know this doesn't end as you want it to," I hissed as he began to move in earnest. His every thrust was meant to drive home his meaning, his dominance and ownership over my pleasure. I screamed as my body unfurled, coming undone around his thickness as he lowered his mouth to my throat and sank his fangs deep into the sore tissue. His first pull of my blood sent me over the edge, violently bucking against him and his driving cock. I murmured his name as I buried my fingers into his silken hair, holding him to me as he fucked me hard and steady, keeping me lost in the pleasure he delivered.

He didn't stop feeding, not even when my hands lost their hold and I whimpered from blood loss. His cock hammered into my cunt, taking everything I had to give as he left me boneless, barely conscious of my surroundings.

"Conner," I moaned as he pulled back, staring down at me as I fought the blackness he had pushed me into. My hands searched for him before dropping to the bed. He'd done it on purpose, I realized too late.

"Sleep, Avery," he growled and stiffened above me, moaning as his mouth brushed against mine, painting my lips red with the blood that covered his.

I was barely conscious when he'd finished fucking me. My hands were lifted, placed in thick metal cuffs before my legs followed the same punishment. The covers were removed, exposing my nakedness to his greedy eyes and I fought the pull to give in to nothingness that promised a respite from the pain and emotional turbulence that danced over my subconscious. Hands touched my naked flesh, pushing through the wet folds as he bent over, pushing his tongue through the slick mess he'd created.

"You're so fucking beautiful," he growled gutturally, staring down at me, eyes skimming over every curve as if he was imprinting it to memory. My knees were lifted, blankets were pushed beneath them, and then someone else was in the room. "Do it," he stated.

"She's very pretty and exposed, Con, is she for me?" a deep voice chuckled as a growl exploded from Conner, along with scuffling of feet. "Fucking chill out, dick, it was a joke. I know she is the one thing you won't ever share. You're sure this is what you want?"

"She's mine, and she isn't fucking leaving here. I'll go to war to keep her, so fucking get on with it."

"They will come for her," the other male said. "She's one of the oldest witches alive, and they will fight to get her back. If she fights us to go, I doubt magic will assist us in keeping her here. Her magic is a lot stronger than mine, Conner, and darker. She's created from one of the purest and oldest bloodlines. I know we've come a long way since you were born, but there are lines they still don't cross. You breeding her is going to be one of them considering what you both are, and what it could mean if it happens."

"Do it, Luca. I've tasted her, and I know she was created for me and me alone. I've known, ever since I pulled her from the pile of dying orphans where I found her, that she was mine. I tried to protect her, to shield myself from what I knew she was, and it cost me everything. I won't give her back, ever. Just do the fucking binding spell, now."

"No," I uttered through heavy lips and a tongue that felt useless and heavy in my mouth. "Conner," I whispered as stars erupted behind eyelids that refused to open. Luca was a witch, but from which coven I didn't know. He was powerful, and yet he seemed to be working willingly with Conner, which explained how he had managed the spell to create an eclipse.

"Sleep," Conner demanded roughly.

"This won't work like you think it is going to. Avery will fight it because that fight is ingrained in her genetic makeup. She isn't from this time; her line is not watered down like most of ours are now. She is a purebred bitch; you might as well try mating with a fucking unicorn because it would be more open to a forced mating than she will ever be. You want my advice? Keep her; put her in chains and keep her as a pet, but don't fucking breed her. Bury the bitch so deep that no one knows you have her, and neuter the magic running through her veins. Mating with her though, will be a fucking mess."

"I didn't ask for your opinion or advice. I told you to bind her to me so that she is mine. Now do it before she wakes up and fights it. Avery is strong, very strong. I know because I'm the one who taught her to use the magic that pulses through her veins. I have watched her grow into a woman, and I was the first man to show her what it meant to be one. I will not allow her to leave here, so do as you were told, now."

I felt my stomach churning with what his words meant. Vampires had mates, and Conner had foregone tasting my blood because we'd long suspected that I was his mate because of the unnatural relationship we had. I was the Queen to his King, and yet that was forbidden. Not to mention that he had been sixth in line to the throne before I'd murdered those who had stood in his way of reaching it. If he did this, I'd be his in every way he wanted, and everything inside of me would fight to help him make it so. That would be an issue when it came time to leave here.

I turned my head, staring into his pretty eyes as I felt the magic in the room thicken. My flesh puckered against it, sending goosebumps over my skin as he leaned in, kissing my lips, I uttered his name. His fingers skimmed my belly, drawing absent circles over it as the witch in the room continued speaking even though I was beyond hearing it. Conner had drained me to the brink of death to leave me powerless. He was trying to mate with me. He planned to keep me, by force, by blood right, and if he succeeded, not even the coven could argue his right. Mates were a law unto their own rules, and nowadays, you didn't dare try to break them up.

Something warm was pushed against my stomach as Conner pulled back, opening his wrist which he held above my mouth, dripping blood into it. I swallowed, drawn to the coppery substance that I'd once been an addict of. Vampire blood healed, but it also did a lot more for witches than it would for mortals. In my veins, he was an aphrodisiac that drove me wild, but that wasn't the problem. It was when our blood combined that everything went horribly wrong.

The first taste created warmth within me. The second created a storm of need that had my hips rocking for what only he could give me. I fought the chains to reach him, to assuage the growing need that curled in my belly as hunger for more of his essence gnawed at me.

"Take her blood," Luca ordered.

The bed dipped against Conner's body weight. His mouth skimmed my throat, and I growled with need as his hand curled around my neck, bending it to give him unhindered access to my vein. Pain rushed through me as his fangs pushed through my flesh, then pleasure exploded through me. My body trembled as he sucked against my throat, running his tongue over the flesh as he fed deeply from me. My cunt wept, needing him to touch me in the ways a man touched a woman and the moment his fingers swept over the sensitive nub, I screamed as pleasure took control and my body succumbed to his touch.

"Conner, stop, she's already mated, pushing this could make her go insane," Luca whispered thickly, not immune to watching us fuck.

Conner pulled his bite from my vein and stared down at me, his eyes heavy with lust as he watched me squirming with an orgasm that refused to release me. Words were jumbled, my aching flesh hummed with the aftershocks of his touch, and blood pooled behind my head as I stared, unseeing at the ceiling.

"Impossible," he growled. "I am the only vampire who has taken her," he hissed as he pushed his hand through the slick folds, gliding his thumb to my flesh before one finger entered me, and then another. I slipped into oblivion as yet another orgasm took me over the edge.

"The amulet, it is spelled against us removing it I'm guessing?" Luca asked.

"Yeah, but why it is, I have no idea."

"She's immortal, but she's also very much mated, Conner. My guess is, that amulet is covering her mating mark and protecting her from the coven finding out she is mated to an enemy. The only way to know for sure would be to do a memory spell or try to remove the amulet to see what it is preventing us from discovering. You'd have to drink the spell, then her, to figure out what she did, and to whom she is mated. Being she is so old, she could have been mated centuries ago, which, as you know, tends to wane the bond over time. You're sure you didn't mate with her when you were fucking her before?" he asked carefully.

"I think I would know if I'd mated Avery. I sure as fuck wouldn't have been able to walk away from her if I had been. I left her with my father to keep it from happening. I assure you, I wanted nothing else than to be mated to her. She was everything to me, and back then, it would have been a death sentence if it had happened. She was already being hunted by covens for being in our hive. I released her to be free from me, Luca, to breed with her own kind to have the child she craved. I sheltered her, and she took everything from me."

"You did what you had to do, and no one foresaw what she would do in her anger. You're enemies by blood and law, and it is a miracle she ever allowed you to get close to her. Back then it was a different world, a law unto itself that your coupling was more than forbidden. Had she been caught with your mark on her, she'd have been burned at the stake. You'd have been given a traitor's death, and neither one of you would have been alive today. Don't carry that guilt, Conner. You released her, and she took everything from you. You're not wrong for wanting to punish her. The hive demands she pays for her crimes and not even the witches can argue that she pays for them. They can argue you mating her, as she carries centuries of their secrets within her. I will brew the spell, but I have to warn you, it will make you feel what she felt, and if she endured anything horrible, you will feel all of it."

"I will also know why she took everything from

me," Conner said with a thickness filling his tone that sent a ripple of pain through me. He wouldn't ever see me as he had before that day. No one would if they knew the truth of the demons that haunted my nightmares.

"I'll see what I can figure out on that amulet as well. There has to be a way to remove it and figure out what it is for."

"Do that," he said as his hand skimmed over my cheek, turning my sightless eyes to his. His mouth brushed over mine, kissing unmoving lips as his forehead touched mine. "I need to know the truth of what happened. I need to know if she was planted to destroy us. If she was, if this has all been some kind of plan to get to my father, I will rip her apart and bury her around the world to send a message to the witches that we will not allow such an atrocity ever to occur again."

"Do you love her?" Luca asked.

"Since the first moment those pretty green eyes looked up at me as if I'd hung the fucking moon for her. I loved her enough to let her go, and that love destroyed us. There hasn't been a single day that has passed that I have not wished for her to be by my side or with me. I need to know the truth, so I can either end her life or begin it anew with her, Luca. I need to know she wasn't planted to destroy me."

"And if she was?" he asked.

"Then she will die by my hand, and I will show the world that I have no mercy against those who trespass against my hive. If she was, then I do not deserve to be King. If she was placed in my path and I fell for it, I will vacate my throne and allow Mayhem to ascend to King of the hive. I will go to ground and sleep until I am ready to rise."

"Mayhem isn't ready to be King. He's a fucking menace to the female population. He'd spend his time doing nothing but wrecking uteruses and sleeping his way through the damn continent. Royal is too twisted to even consider as a King, Addison isn't interested in ruling, and the hive follows the bloodline. Your bloodline. You are one of a very few born vampires. The four of you lead us together, and if you go to ground, this entire hive will fall apart. You know that."

"If Avery was placed into my path to bring down my father and the hive, I don't think they'd stay together either way, Luca. I fell for my enemy, and I fell hard and fast. I watched her grow from a dirty street urchin into a woman. I brought her into our ranks because I couldn't stomach the idea of her dying in that dirty fucking alleyway with the others who had perished. Avery wasn't a decoy to me; she was my mate even though I didn't allow it to happen. I have never looked at a woman and not compared them to her. Fuck, Luca, I moved the entire hive out of England to these fucking mountains because I can't let her go. Do you know what it took for me to hand her to my father? I was drained, placed into the ground, and given the eternal rest of the dead for an entire year before Addison and Mayhem brought me back from it. I had to be mindless, unable to go after her to let her go. So she can't be mated, because she is mine. She's always been mine. We both knew what we were, and we were careful to not conceive a child, or for me to feed from her vein because that is all it would have taken for her to receive my mating mark, of that I am sure. That would have been a death sentence, one my father assured me he would carry out for both of us should it happen. I need to know why she murdered them, but more than that, I need to know what happened after I left her with my father. He was to wipe away her memories of me, of us, from her mind and release her to the Americas. Something went wrong, or it was what she was placed there to do, and I wasn't there to stop it. I have to know what happened and I'll do whatever it takes to get that information."

"I will prepare the spell and see what I can discover about the magic holding that amulet in place. I fear she may have been planted, and if she were, you would be forced to murder the woman you love, Conner. You have not stopped loving her, not even with what she did to your family. If she is mated to another, what happens then?"

"I feel her, Luca. I feel that girl so fucking deep inside of me that I fear I am her mate. Maybe we fucked up and I claimed her, or maybe she found another when she first left, but there's been no vampire around her since she left me that I am aware. I only lost her for twenty years, and in that time, I can't know what happened, so maybe it is possible. I've known where she was since the moment she crawled out of the shadows. I do know that she didn't go outside after sundown, and never before sunrise. I followed her here from England, and I ripped apart any male who looked at her with lust. I thought she'd taken lovers, but after last night, and what I discovered as I fucked her, I don't think she has taken a lover in over two hundred years. Tell me, how is that even possible? They breed bloodlines like we do, and yet Avery wasn't lying, and she is one they'd want to breed for power. Yet it was as if she was a virgin again last night, she had a fucking hymen, and she fucked me better than any trained whore could have ever hoped to please me. I had to feed her blood to keep her from bleeding out after I'd fucked her."

"That doesn't seem possible. Cheveron witches, in general, are too powerful to leave dormant, and I don't think they'd let that go. They would have had men trying for her hand and bed often, and the elders would have demanded she be bred to bring more of her line into this world."

"Nothing with her makes sense, other than her being here with me. She's not leaving here, not even if I have to slaughter witches and start a war," Conner said with enough anger in his tone that I knew without seeing his eyes that he meant it.

"She isn't worth starting a war over," Luca uttered.

"You're wrong. Avery is worth it to me. My father knew it too; that was why he forced me to sleep. It's why he had to corner me and make me see what would happen if I mated with her. I was willing to go to war for her then, and I am willing to do it now. Find me a way to keep her without starting this war, or give me the proof I need to make it easier to let her leave this world and have the peace she desires. Do it quickly, because the witches are coming and I will murder every last fucking one of them before I hand her back to them."

CHAPTER EIGHT

I'd woken up alone in his room. The tub had been filled and beckoned me invitingly. He'd filled it to the brim with steaming hot water that rose over the rim, spilling the delicate scent of peonies into the air thickly. I settled my wary frame into the sudsy water, letting the tears slip free as memories of another lifetime filled my mind with the scent that filled the air as I bathed.

His touch was my heroin, a drug that I couldn't get enough of. I'd been lost the moment he'd first kissed me at sixteen, but the day he'd taken me for the first time, I'd wanted nothing else, and no one else, and so he'd promised never to allow another to touch me as he did. Not even his father had swayed him from that promise.

I sunk beneath the water, listening as the door opened and closed before I slipped from the water's embrace to stare into the shadows, but he wasn't there. Instead, Amery sat on a chair, watching me through a cold stare.

"He is going to kill you, you know. It is all the hive speaks about." she buffed her nails on her sundress, lifting green eyes to watch me as she spoke icily. "You're nothing to him; he doesn't even care about you."

"Good," I shrugged as I hugged my knees to my chest and watched her through my lashes. "And you came here to tell me I'm in danger, or to convince yourself that I am not a threat?"

"You're nothing to me, less than nothing to the King," she hissed as she stood up, walking to the sidebar to pour herself a drink.

Watching her as she poured the drink, I replayed what she'd said over in my head. She spun around to stare at me as she brought the glass to her lips, drinking deeply. There was malice rolling off of her in waves. Waves that bespoke of hatred and anger for being removed from his bed, but that was something I could work with.

"If I am nothing, then why am I in his bed and you're in the feeder quarters? Or better yet, Amery, why do you look like me?" I asked, noting the subtle differences between us.

"I look nothing like you. I was also here first, so I'm above you, bitch," she hissed before she tipped the glass back, polishing it off for courage.

"Okay, so you came in here to size me up. Are you finished?"

"You're not even pretty. You have nothing to lure him away from me. He hasn't fed from another since I was purchased, and I am the only one he fucks. As I said, you're nothing to him. He will continue to summon me because I soothe him, and we have something good together. You will be dead soon enough, and everything will go back to as it was before you were brought here."

"Except the part where he plans to keep me as his feeder," I said offhandedly as I rose from the water, showing her the red, swollen flesh he'd used until the early morning hours, even as his sleep began to take him into nothingness where vampires slumbered. I'd felt him pulling me closer, securing me as he spoke to the other man before he'd left.

"You lie, whore. It is all everyone talks about. You murdered his father, and for that, he will demand your head. It is the law to kill those who betray the hive!" she hissed as she turned, refilling her glass as I slipped out of the tub.

Green eyes traced my steps as I moved to the bed, naked. I hadn't been given clothes, which I was sure hadn't been an accident. Sitting down, I pulled the covers over my nudity, moving my hair to give her a bird's eye view of the bruises on my neck from his endless hours of feeding. She frowned as she took in the small, angry red marks his fangs had left behind.

"He fed from you?" she asked softly as though she was unaffected by it, yet her mottled red complexion gave her away. "He has fed from no other whore since I came to him. What did you do to encourage him?" she demanded.

"I'm not here willingly, so don't assume I am or that I am encouraging any of what is happening to me. I'd prefer to escape him and this place." Bait and hooked, if she fell for it, I'd find a way to escape him and his seductive touches.

I studied her for a moment. Her eyes weren't the same shade as my own, but they were pretty. Her blonde eyebrows gave her dye job away, and I knew it had been done on Conner's request. Her breasts were much larger than mine, but he hadn't ever been impressed with attributes, which she apparently hadn't noticed. Her curves plumped out around her hips, flaring invitingly, even with the unflattering sundress she wore. She was taller than me, not as petite or delicate as I was. I had stopped aging at seventeen, which meant I was tiny compared to others. Luckily, my curves and breasts had formed before then, not that it mattered now anyway. Amery's hair was frayed from being dyed, as well as split at the ends from countless hair products that stunk. Even now, as I stood there, I could smell her overwhelming perfume and products she'd applied.

"You do look a lot like me. I can see where he would be attracted to you. However, I'm sure you noticed when he fucked you so carelessly the other night, he was staring at me, wishing it was me he was fucking." I almost felt bad about goading her into assisting me, but her haughtiness and attitude told me there were countless feeders being abused by this petty bitch in the quarters. "Let me guess, when he fucks you, you can't speak. You wouldn't have my accent, you were born in this era and not in ours. He probably only takes you from behind, as your face is not the same shape as mine either. Stop me if I'm wrong here," I said with a knowing look burning in my eyes because I knew him like I knew the back of my hand, or I had.

"He loves me, and he will never stop. He and I have something special. I will become the Queen, and I will watch him remove your head while I relish it and cheer my King and lover on."

I felt bad over the delusions she suffered, but then

she'd just spoken about my head being removed, and I was sort of attached to it. "You *did*, he punished you for me escaping him and his reach. If I were to escape again, you'd have that part of him back. He won't summon you back into this room as long as I am in his bed. In fact, I doubt he spares you a second thought now that he has what he really wants within his grasp. You were, after all, my stand-in until he could get to me. Were you even born with your name, or did he change that for you too? Much easier to whisper Avery if the whore you're fucking is named Amery. How often did he scream my name instead of yours?" I asked as I climbed from the bed and moved to the sidebar, bypassing her angry stance as I poured myself a drink and tipped it back before grabbing the bottle pointedly and moving back to the bed. The moment before I scrambled back beneath the covers, her eyes dropped to my swollen sex that was still angry red from being used endlessly throughout the night.

"Never, he knew who he was with the entire time. Only when his hands settled around my throat did I allow him to pretend I was you. He *is* mine; he has been since the moment he purchased me from my mother. I come from a long line of prestige feeders that are skilled in areas that most vampires cannot even begin to afford to purchase, let alone own. I am worth more to him than any other whore here, including you. The honor of being his only feeder is widely known in the quarter. I am respected by all because he favors me and only me! You *will* be dead, and who do you think will comfort him when that day comes?"

"I am immortal, so not sure you should hold your

breath on that one. I mean, you said he has not fed from another since he purchased you, and yet he drank from me all night long, and I don't have the same limitations that you, as a mortal, suffer from. I can be drained, but I won't die from it like you would. I also spent last night with him knowing who he was fucking, and it wasn't him pretending he was fucking someone else. So, while you're tooting your horn, there are some things to consider. Also, maybe consider that I don't want to be here, and if I were to leave here, you could go back to being *my* stand-in cunt for the King." I shrugged and lifted the bottle, sipping from it as I watched her turn red with anger.

"He is mine, and I would never help you escape. I am not an idiot. That would end up with me being given a traitor's death. You will lose your worth once he has fucked you out of his system." She crossed her arms, glaring daggers at me.

"Because he has yet to manage that after centuries, also might not want to hold your breath on that one either," I said, slowly turning away from her and dropping the blanket strategically as the bedroom door opened and Conner entered, heat banked in his violet-blue depths as they settled on my naked form.

Those eyes dropped to my exposed breasts greedily. A sinful smile lifted his lips while he walked towards me, not sparing Amery a single glance. I fidgeted with the blanket as he moved towards the only chair in the room, sitting down slowly. His stare moved to Amery before it dismissed her entirely.

"Come to me, imp," he purred thickly. I stood up to do as he had asked when Amery rushed forward, bending down and began to unlace his shoes. He watched her before he lifted his eyes to observe me as I slowly walked towards him. "Get the fuck out, Amery," he growled as his eyes dipped to the swollen flesh he'd abused last night.

"My King, I am here to pleasure you. Use me as you like," she offered in a seductive tone that bordered on desperation.

"Avery, come to me," he said thickly, holding his hand out for me. Stepping over Amery, I straddled his legs while he cupped my cheek while his thumb ran down my jawline before he brushed it over my lips. "I'm ravenous, little witch." His eyes watched me carefully as I pushed my hair away from my neck and offered him my throat, even as my heart thundered with what was coming. He smiled darkly and lifted me, forcing my back against his chest as he turned me in his arms. He parted my legs, running his other hand down my smooth stomach to my apex, pushing his thumb against the sensitive nub there. "You're wet for me. I'm glad to find you more willing to your new part today, imp," he pointed out, and I hissed as his finger pushed into the mess that flooded my core with the images of last night playing through my mind.

"Conner," I uttered hoarsely as he continued toying with me. His mouth touched against my throat, and I moaned huskily as his finger pushed into my sex. He licked my neck, using his tongue to mimic his fingers as he brought me close to the edge of the cliff and left me teetering there. His fangs pushed into my throat as he used his other hand to squeeze one breast before his other hand lifted along with the first to pinch my nipples until I squirmed as pain mingled with pleasure. My moans grew louder, and the storm within me seemed to grow stronger.

Something wet touched my cunt, and I stared down while Conner held my breasts. Amery licked through the mess he had created of me. I stiffened as his tongue closed the wounds and his hands stilled. He pulled me closer, staring down to where she had started fucking me with her mouth. A shiver raced through me as I closed my eyes, turning away from what she was doing to me without my permission and panic rushed through me.

"Amery, get the fuck off of her," he snarled icily. Conner lifted me carefully the moment she raised her head to stare up with my arousal coating her lips. One moment I was in his arms, the next I was in the chair alone, and he held her by her hair, glaring down at her. Amery was forced to stand on her tiptoes as he shook her. "No one fucking touches her, ever! She is mine, whore. You were told to leave; do you prefer to be removed by force, or will you leave on your own?"

"I'm here for your pleasure, Conner," she whimpered as her hands reached for him. He set her on her feet, watching as she struggled to undress him through shaking hands while her wide green eyes wept fat alligator tears.

"Do not ever address me informally, Amery. You are here because you offer me relief, nothing else. You were told to get out," he hissed coldly, watching her struggle. She turned wild eyes towards me where I surveyed them, and I swallowed hard past the uneasiness her desperation made me feel. She dropped her hands and lunged at me with murder in her eyes. She never made it to me. Instead, Conner caught her mid-lunge and threw her back towards the wall where she crumpled to the floor.

"Sire, I am yours," she sobbed brokenly.

"You are *not* mine. Avery is mine, and you just tried to hurt her when she is off-limits and here as my prisoner. Leave now, before I take your head from your shoulders or do something worse yet. You betrayed me and should face a traitor's death, but I think not. I think you will be given to the men to assuage their egos at never being able to touch you until now."

"No, please! I will do whatever you want, take whatever you want from me, but don't share me. I will be Avery for you again, please, my King. I only thought to please you and your new bedmate."

Snot ran down her face with tears that drove home memories of another broken girl I'd watched falling apart with no hope of survival. Before I thought better of it, I grabbed Conner's arm and pulled him to me, kissing him with everything I had in me to give her time to escape. His hands lifted me, pulling me against him as I wrapped my arms around his neck in desperation. I eyed her as he moved me towards the bed, watching as she rose from the floor to stare at us as he ripped at his clothes, unwilling to wait the time it would take him to strip out of them. Seconds passed by before he was driving into my body as I continued devouring him, unable to stop myself from putting in every emotion I had felt since he'd left me in possession of the hive into the kiss. It was anger, betrayal, desperation, and more that I'd never allowed out until now. It was everything I'd felt when he'd left me, and everything I'd never planned to show him, all wrapped into one kiss.

"Avery," he growled as he lifted his mouth from mine, staring down at me before he turned, watching the door close behind his whore. "You think to save her?" he asked, lifting up as he brought me with him.

"No one deserves to be handed to the hive to be abused," I uttered as I leaned my forehead against his. "Now move, Conner," I hissed as he picked me up and slammed me down on his cock. "Harder," I demanded.

"I remember a girl who liked it soft and slow," he replied huskily.

"That girl died when you left her to the hive, now fuck me," I countered and felt him stiffen.

"Who did you mate with, Avery?" he asked harshly. His bluish purple eyes studied me as he held me still, unable to move as he remained inside of me.

"I am unmated," I whispered thickly.

"Don't fucking lie to me," he demanded as he picked me up and tossed me over his shoulder onto the bed. "I had a witch try to bind you to me as my mate last night, and he couldn't because you are already fucking mated to someone else. I want to know whom you allowed to claim you so I can hang his fucking head above my throne so the world knows you are mine and mine alone."

"You tried to bind me to you by force?" I asked as I sat up, staring at him as he paced before the bed, naked and hard in his glorious anger. "Why would you even want that?"

"So that I can fuck you whenever I want to," he snapped. "So that you would look at me like you used to look at me, and kiss me like I am your fucking air,

Avery. So that when the witches come to argue for your life, they won't be able to because it belongs to me!"

"And I'd be what to you, Conner, your whore?"

"My whore? What do you think you are now? You're a prisoner who murdered the fucking King of the England Vampires! You are mine to do as I please with until I decide otherwise! You won't give me a reason for slaughtering them, and I have asked until I am blue in the face. Soon enough, I will know what you did and why you did it. There will be nothing you can keep hidden from me, Avery."

"What is that supposed to mean?" I demanded as he searched my eyes.

"It means I'm done fucking around and asking what happened. I deserve the truth."

"*You* deserve the truth? You don't deserve shit! You left me in a hive with men who had been told that they would never be allowed to touch me, and then left me with them. What the fuck do you think happened?"

"Stop lying," he snarled as he paused in front of me. "My father wouldn't have allowed it to happen!"

"Your father was the first to fuck me! Then your brothers joined in the fun, and then the men. You want to know what happened, Conner. They destroyed me. They took turns tearing me apart, and at day, they'd feed me your blood so that I'd be so high that I *liked* it! I didn't know who was fucking me anymore. I was the whore! I was their whore, and they made damn sure I never forgot where I belonged. Even worse, I begged them for it. I begged for the blood that made my mind think I was with you and I let them do whatever the hell they wanted to me so I could survive them. There, now you know what they did to me."

"My brothers wouldn't have hurt you. My father helped me keep you safe from the others. I don't buy your lies anymore, witch," he shouted as he grabbed my arm and, ripping me from the bed, he walked me back to the cross. I hit against it with my back, crying out as his anger slithered over my flesh. "They loved you as much as your own parents could have. How fucking dare you say anything less about them."

"Believe whatever you want, Conner. I don't need you to believe it, but when you offered to give Amery to your men who have been denied the use of her cunt, what did you think they would do with her? Did you assume they'd buy her flowers and line up to date her or abuse her until she no longer could tell the difference between who used her body?" I asked softly as tears streaked down my cheeks.

"Shut your fucking mouth or I will shut it for you, whore," he hissed vehemently. My eyes closed at the name he used as everything inside of me screamed. My mouth clamped shut as I dropped my eyes, staring at the floor with no expression, no emotion as I'd learned to do long ago. He secured my arms and my ankles before he stepped back towards me. "Look at me."

I wouldn't, I'd find a way to escape him, and I'd get the others away from the murdering bastards who thought we belonged leashed and at heel. I'd find a way to survive because it was what I did. I survived to watch the world change around me, to watch those I loved die slowly before my eyes. I went on, even when I shouldn't have.

"I said, look at me," he demanded as his fingers

bit into my flesh, lifting my chin. I opened my eyes, staring blankly into his. "I gave you the world. I gave you immortality and a way to live at my side, and this is how you repay me? You lie to me about what happened in that place of death; you make up vile lies about my family, and for what? *Pity?* Do you think even if I believed what you said, that I would feel sorry for you? You are beneath me, just as my father said you were. You and your kind deal in lies and treachery and make up lies about what happened to make yourself look better. I'm not some little prince who is besotted by you anymore, Avery. I'm the King, and I demand answers for what you did. If I find out you were planted to do what you did, not even all the witches of this world are going to be enough to protect you from me."

"Just end it, Conner," I whispered softly, watching him glaring through slanted eyes at me. "Kill me, please. You stole death from me. Give it to me now. End it here, right here, right now. *Do it!*" I screamed as I shook with the memories and horror of what I'd been forced to escape from because he'd made me immortal, and only he could end my life. "I wish for it, every morning when I wake up, and every night when I go to sleep. I pray for death, so just fucking do it already and be done with this."

"Never. Never, little witch. You are mine as you promised to be for all time. I may not even end it if I discover you betrayed me from the beginning. There are fates worse than death."

"I'm very aware of them. I lived through them."

"You have no idea of the things we can do to you," he uttered softly.

"There's nothing you can do to me that hasn't already been done, Conner. I am good with pain, and I know what death looks like. I have felt it all, thanks to you and your family. When I said I'd wished you had left me in the garbage to die, I wish you had to spare me everything I have endured. You think you can scare me with pain, or the threat of it? Try me. Throw me to the hive and let them play with me, show me what a good King you are. I'll be okay with them, fuck, I may even like it."

CHAPTER NINE

My arms burned from being suspended for days, and my legs felt unattached as they hung uselessly below me. Conner came and went as he pleased, touching me, driving me to the brink of madness as he touched and used me like I was nothing more than his personal toy. He never spoke to me, or about me, and I never tried to engage him in conversation either. I had stopped responding to his touches last night, only allowing it to play out and move when he demanded it, like a machine built for his pleasure.

I was lost in the memories I'd buried long ago, so deeply embedded into the blackness of my mind that I'd almost been able to pretend they didn't exist. Now they seemed to seep through my pores, clawing through the surface of my mind as I slept, haunting my dreams. Exhaustion made them worsen, made them dominant in my mind as I was left with my demons while he played King below in the hall he'd created to mirror his father's throne room.

Today, however, he watched me from the shadows

of the room, studying me as I waited for him to play with me. The silence haunted me, it unnerved me until I was sure I'd lose it and begin screaming. His father had kept me in a dark room for months, holding me there in chains until I'd never thought to look upon the sun or feel it heating my face again.

Conner stood, slowly moving towards me in nothing more than a pair of loose-fitting jeans that hugged his hips. I didn't gaze into his eyes, nor look upon the face I'd once loved. I stared at his feet, giving him the submission he craved, and even when he demanded it, I didn't look up. I'd learned this lesson from his father and brothers, to look up meant abuse would be given, or an inch of flesh would be taken. To these creatures, I was nothing. I was less than nothing, and an enemy that refused to be used against her own kind held only one use. Those were the options Grigori had given me that day. Submit and be used as a weapon, or die a million deaths at his hand, since I couldn't be killed outright because of what Conner, his son, had made me into.

I'd prayed for death, begged the Gods to let me join them on the other side, if there was one. I'd begged the Goddess to give me mercy, to end the suffering I endured daily as I refused to submit to Grigori's will. I'd begged them to take me to Conner, but everyone had told me he'd known my fate, that he had agreed to it before he'd walked away from me, leaving me to their mercy for which they had none.

"Look at me, Avery," he growled. When I didn't, he grabbed my chin, lifting my eyes to his, and yet I didn't see him. His eyes searched my face before he dropped his hold on it and let his hands lower to my naked breasts, tweaking my nipples as he watched me. "You brought this on yourself, waif. My father knew how much you meant to me, and he was a good man. I couldn't let you go back to the witches knowing everything about us. You were born my enemy, and I couldn't trust you not to become it again when I'd let you go."

My heart hammered painfully against my ribcage as I listened to his version of our relationship. To him, his father was a King among men, and his word was his bond. He had loved him, holding him on an ivory pedestal. Of course, he hadn't been forced to learn the truth of the monster that had created him, but I had. I hadn't been able to ignore the truth, nor the strength of his hands around my throat as he'd fucked me. I'd been unable to ignore the real monster that Conner had been spared from seeing.

"You have nothing to say to me, waif?" he demanded softly as he bent down, releasing my feet before standing up to free my hands. The moment I was released, I fell to the floor, unable to catch myself before my mind realized I would need to.

I didn't rise from the floor. Instead, I crawled into position and knelt as his feet with my head held down in a submissive position. He knelt in front of me, placing two fingers beneath my chin before lifting my face to stare into my eyes.

"Tell me the truth. Tell me my father didn't rape you and you just wanted my pity," he hissed.

"Your father didn't rape me. I just wanted your pity," I replied, telling him what he'd said to say.

"Fucking mean it!" he shouted, and I flinched, recoiling as I placed my head at his feet with my ass in the air, submitting. "What the fuck are you doing?" he growled.

"What a good whore does, master," I uttered barely above a whisper. "I am whatever you wish me to be, and will do whatever you wish of me. I am nothing and no one. Use me as you wish to."

"Get the fuck up," he hissed through his teeth.

I rose to my feet even though my thighs burned from being suspended for days. My eyes remained on his bare feet as I struggled to stay upright. He walked around me, staring at my prone position. He silently removed his belt, slipping it free of his waist before he slipped it around my neck. I tensed but remained still as he tightened it.

"I'm going to guess whoever the fuck mated with you liked it rough and that you played along with it to please him. So show me what you like, Avery. Show me how to fuck you right. The little waif I knew, she didn't like to be manhandled, she liked it gentle and slow. She liked to feel me stretching her tight pussy when I fucked it slowly, but you, you want it hard and fast. So, show me what your husband or mate enjoyed, and what you allowed him to do to you."

"I am not married, nor do I have a mate, master," I whispered as he tightened the belt until it began to close off my airway.

"You are mated, or you would be mine right now. How many men have you fucked since I took you to my father and left you?"

"Two hundred and seventy-three men and seventeen women have used me, and I served each well and pleased them greatly, master."

"*Used* you?" he asked hesitantly. *"Women?"*

"There are ways to penetrate a body that doesn't include having a cock. I learned to take whatever they gave me or put into me however they chose to do so. What would you like to use on me, master? I can accommodate many things, and I enjoy the pain it gives."

"Stop it, Avery," he warned as he pulled me closer, catching me as my legs gave out. His hand lifted my chin, finding the tears swimming in my eyes, and he frowned deeply, disturbed by my words.

"Tell me how you want me to be, and I will be it," I whispered thickly. "Tell me how to act, and I will. Tell me how to pleasure you, and I will be the best whore you have ever had. You want me to tell you that everything was amazing when I was with your father, I will. I will do whatever it takes to survive. I am *witch*. My goal is to survive whatever happens to me, no matter how deeply it scars my soul. To endure and survive until the coven comes to free me."

"Don't you fucking recite that shit ass mantra to me," he snapped angrily. "You said it to me for weeks as I fed you my blood to bring you back from the grave. Day after day, I held you in my arms, not allowing your weak body to leave mine for fear your pulse would fucking stop. Me, Avery, I held you through the storm, and I cared alone if you lived or died. Not your fucking coven, never them. You whispered it so many times that I still hear it when I sleep. You're not a whore. You've never been one, nor will you ever be one. No matter what the fuck I choose to call you, we both know the fucking truth."

"Okay," I agreed, nodding to him without lifting my head.

"You're not fucking docile either, so stop pretending to be. Where's the fucking firecracker who loved to argue with me? Where the fuck did that girl go?"

"You killed her," I said gently as I dropped to my knees and waited for him to issue an order. My hands folded in front of me, my head bowed as my spine arched into the position his father had loved. I waited for the order, to either be shared or given to whoever had pleased the King the most today.

"Get up!" he growled and stepped back, watching me as I once again struggled to rise from the ground; the exhaustion of raising and lowering into the position sapped my strength, and yet I would rise because I would survive this too.

"I told you, I learned where I belong and how to please my masters. That is what you are now, right? I am your prisoner just as I was your father's. You plan to fuck me whenever you want, so did your father. Will you share me too? I find that with enough of your blood in my system, I don't care who hurts me or who takes me. You're right; they didn't rape me, Conner. They didn't need to, they just fed me your blood, and I did whatever they wanted. It wasn't the sex that bothered me though; it was what they did to me after it had worn off. Do you know what your hive did to the witches they captured? How they cut them apart to rid the parts that could cast? They take their points from them, all of them."

"You don't have a single fucking scar on you," he said, grabbing my hair and pulling me to him as he removed the belt from my neck. "You're as perfect as you were the day I walked away from you. Your pretty green eyes may have lost their sparkle, but they're still the most beautiful thing I have ever looked into. Your saucy little tongue, it still brushes against mine with a shyness that makes me ache to feel it. Your silky midnight curls that frame your perfect heart-shaped face is still as soft as it was when I held you the night I made you into a woman. Your skin is smooth, still perfect against mine. So tell me, Avery, how much fucking torture could you have endured after I left you?" he demanded harshly.

"Just because you can't see it doesn't mean it isn't there," I said as I shoved him away from me. "You want me, feed me your blood, and I'll do whatever you want. Put me back in chains if you're done with me for the night, a good whore waits in silence to be fucked. I don't need to listen to your fucking drivel when my cunt needs to be filled." It was crude and the last thing I wanted, and yet he wanted the truth, but he couldn't handle the truth of what I'd endured—shit, most days I couldn't handle it either.

"Is that what you want, my blood?" he asked.

"That is the price to use the whores, is it not? Come on, princeling, give it to me and show me what you got. Feed me, and I'll rock your world." I stared him down as he glared at me, but his finger rose, slicing through his pectoral muscle as his breathing intensified with his need, his anger driving him.

I stepped closer, licking my lips as I slid my tongue over his chest before biting my lip open to mix them, growling loudly as the blood touched my tongue. I sucked against his flesh and his hands captured my head, holding me there as my mouth sucked against the wound greedily. My hands stroked his sides, and before I knew his intention, his hands pulled my mouth away from the source of his blood, kissing me. He picked me up, moving towards the bed as my hands found his hair, yanking his mouth from mine. I stared at him, unseeing.

"Conner," I whispered breathlessly as I let him drop us to the bed before I pushed away, working his pants to get them undone. The moment they were, I stroked his cock slowly before I licked down the length and then back up again, wetting it for my throat before I took him entirely into my mouth. I took him all, bobbing against it even though no air reached my lungs as he sealed my airway. His frenzied noises only emboldened me as I swallowed until light exploded behind my eyes as my lungs burned. Not even when he pulled at my hair did I stop sucking or fucking him with my throat. His blood, when combined with mine, made it impossible for me to stop or feel anything. The only need I held was to please him and him alone. It was as if I'd been given drugs that numbed my mind and body and created an addiction to please him.

"Avery," he whispered as he pulled my hair, forcing my head back.

I stared at him, seeing through him to the ghosts that stood around us. I rose from the bed to my knees, crawling over him as he watched me. "I can do better, master. Let me please you," I uttered past the burning in my throat.

"What the fuck is wrong with you?" he demanded huskily.

My mouth landed on the cut that threatened to close, needing more to forget the pain that haunted me. I kissed it before using my blunt teeth to open the wound as I took from him what he gave freely. He hissed as I bit into his flesh. My cunt slid over his smooth cock, riding the rigid edge to please him. He pulled me from his blood, dropping his eyes to my bloodied mouth, realizing it wasn't just his blood coating them as his blood healed the wound on my lip. It was our blood mixed together that worked against me. It always had, as if when it mixed, it turned my body against me and made me into whatever they wanted me to become, only it had never happened until after he'd left me. I'd never had the combination until after I'd been beaten and had his blood forced down my throat.

His lips crushed against mine and I lifted, letting him feel me as the moan ripped through my throat, filling his mouth. I bucked against him, drinking him in, kissing him with everything I had ever felt for him, giving him everything I had as I rode him until he captured my head, staring into sightless eyes as I did what he wanted, what he craved.

He paused, releasing my head to still my swaying hips. I ground myself over him, coming undone while everything inside of me collided and crashed into a cataclysmic event that rocked through me. His hands held me still, watching me until I floated back to earth as the high started to fade and leave me with the reality of what I had done.

"What the fuck was that?" he demanded thickly. "Avery, what the hell just happened?"

"Our blood, yours and mine," I whispered hoarsely. "I need more, and then you can hurt me."

"Jesus Christ," he muttered as he watched me. "I've

never given you my blood mixed with yours."

"Your father did," I whispered roughly. "He beat me, and then fed me your blood. I love us. It's like heroin when we are mixed together. It makes me feel nothing, and every cock I take is yours. It's perfect, isn't it?"

"That is impossible, he wouldn't have had my blood there," he snapped.

"Mayhem brought it to him," I said offhandedly as I lay back on the bed. "Come with me, Conner."

"Avery, something is wrong with you," he groaned and dropped his head into his hands as he sat on the edge of the bed.

"I need you, my prince."

"I'm the fucking King, remember? You slaughtered my father and any male that stood in my way of the throne."

"I know, but they hurt me. They took my parts away. So I took their fucking souls. I'm sorry."

"You're *sorry*?" he hissed as he turned and looked at me where I played with myself to lure him to me, needing more of his delicious blood. "Look at you, you're fucking high!"

"Mmm, and you're not playing with me," I laughed with an alluring smile, reaching for him as he watched me. "Come touch me, I can make you feel good."

"You're not willing, you're drugged. It doesn't make sense. Nothing you're saying makes sense. Mayhem was with me, guarding me as I slumbered, Avery. I slept to let you go, and he was charged with safeguarding me by our father."

"Fuck me," I begged. "I need more, please. I'll do whatever you want, you can hurt me too. Just give it to me, please!"

"No, no, I don't want you drugged when I fuck you. I want you to want me, and not like this. You never needed to be drugged or forced to want me. Something isn't right," he uttered as he left the bed, withdrawing his phone from his discarded jeans. "It's me; get the fuck up here, now. Something is wrong with Avery. She's high as fuck… No, I didn't fucking drug her. She cut her lip and drank my blood, and now she wants me. Yeah, I know it doesn't make sense. I'm aware, get the fuck up here, Luca. Now," he shouted into the phone as I pouted, running my hands down my smooth stomach.

CHAPTER TEN

Conner

I stared at her slumbering form, needing to be buried within her and yet knowing whatever the fuck just happened wasn't right. She whimpered in her sleep, and everything inside of me wished to know what was happening in her dreams. My Avery never submitted, she never cowered before me. She never fucking bowed her head to any man, so what the fuck had changed her?

"She's highly drugged," Luca said as he waved his hand over her slumbering form, and yet her eyes were wide open but unfocused, staring into nothingness as if she was dead. "You know the myth about mates who are linked on a higher level than any other kind, right?"

"Fated soulmates? The ones that withstand time and place to always come back to one another, those myths?" I snorted impatiently as my balls ached to find release in her tight, welcoming cunt.

"That particular myth, yes," he agreed as his lime-green eyes held mine as his dark hair hung loosely over his broad shoulders.

"Avery isn't my mate, remember? We couldn't even force it to happen."

"No, *I* couldn't force *her* to be your mate. She is mated, but I can't sense another male on her, no one but you. I'm saying she may be yours and you may not have realized it, and I sure as hell can't tell you if she is your mate. I've heard that if a soulmate endures trauma, and can't sense her mate, it can sever their bond. It would be her anchor, and without being able to reach into the universe and feel you, say if you were in the eternal slumber of your kind, she'd assume you had been dead, and the link would then sever as if you were actually dead. I'm saying that maybe something happened, and you weren't there, and your bond died with hers. She'd be technically mated until she died, and her soul would be reborn to find yours. She can't die though, so who the fuck knows what her soul is doing, ya know? Hear me out here, vampires mate by a blood bond, but she's a witch. We still don't know dick about the two breeds being able to bond or mate, so I can't say if you are her actual mate, but I don't see her screaming anyone else's name, do you?"

"You're saying she was traumatized and reached for her mate, but he wasn't available, because she sure as shit wasn't reaching for me," I snorted, crossing my arms to study her sleeping form. I wanted to know if she was mated, and if she was, who was he, and how could he manage to stay away from her this long. I tried, and it had been the hardest thing I'd ever done in my entire life. It felt as if I'd ripped my own heart out and squeezed it when I walked away from her.

Avery had been a weakness since the first moment she tried to save me from the plague. She had tried to protect me from herself, while she was dying. She pushed me away, whispering about the Black Death, and that not even the angels like *me* were immune to its hold. I stood in that dark alleyway, watching her as she struggled to work the spell to save me from the plague, or one she thought might have worked to protect me. She had been so innocent, so pure and untouched by the hatred the other witches felt for my kind. I scooped her tiny form up from the pile of dead bodies they'd thrown her on top of and took her home.

In my room, I found my father's witch Hemlock, and offered him the one thing he craved the most. I gave him pure, born vampire blood, only *if* he could save her life. I spent months feeding her my blood, only for the plague to come back, and each time, death got closer to stealing the little waif from me. He worked a spell to make her immortal, like me. When I was sure she was safe, and I felt her heart thundering in perfect harmony with mine, I murdered him to keep the secret of her immortality safe and guarded.

I watched her for an entire year before I found the little imp standing in the shadows of my room, watching me feed from one of the whores I used. Her eyes lit up every time I slammed into the woman I fucked, watching, learning what I enjoyed as I took them. The first time, she entered my room at fourteen, slipping in before I could bring in my dinner, she'd stripped her body bare as I watched from the shadows. Tiny hands shook with fear of the unknown; her perky breasts had yet to finish growing. She had slipped beneath the covers naked, waiting for me to discover her there when I returned. I never went to bed that night. Instead, I watched her until the dawn rose and forced me to slip from the room to find shelter from the light that bathed her iridescent skin with its warm kiss.

It became a game we played. Avery watched me fuck, and I watched her bathe, so fucking vulnerable that I could have taken her at any time I wanted. I wouldn't though, because her innocence drew me to her, and the way she looked at me, the way her eyes danced with love, kept me her prisoner more than any chains would ever manage.

The day she turned sixteen, nothing could stop me from claiming her after she had come with my name escaping her pretty pink lips. We'd both danced around it for years, but I felt her so fucking deep within me that she was a drug, and I would never be able to get enough. I'd been gentle, tender even, which wasn't something I'd ever done before. Avery was my Queen, my heart in human form. I'd given her everything her world couldn't give her and made up for everything she missed from losing her mortal life.

I kept her safe, and she kept me sane. I guarded her from monsters she hadn't even known hunted her. She was a diamond among a pile of rocks, and I knew it from the first moment I found her. Avery was a fucking Cheveron witch, the purest and strongest bloodline any coven had ever known. She was my fucking unicorn, and that drew monsters to her. I slaughtered entire covens who sought to take her from me, who wanted to wield her as a weapon against us. I murdered vampires who thought to touch her, or even glance upon her with lust in their eyes. She spoke to me of love, about creating a forbidden life together, which caught my father's interest. The covenant of coven and vampires had forbidden it, and yet I craved it with her. I relished the thought of creating a child with both her magic and my immortality, one that we would create together. I was warned of what would happen should I proceed, and I pushed her away from me for a time. But she was fucking Avery, my imp that argued anything she thought was right, and to her, we were right, and anything we created together couldn't be wrong. How the fuck did you argue that logic? We were forbidden lovers, and fuck, I loved her so hard and so fast that it was just right. She was mine, and she taught me selfless love was something that couldn't be taken, it had to be given. Then I slaughtered Javier, son to the King of Spain Vampires. It wasn't just a crime; it was treason against the entire vampire covenant. I killed a prince to keep her safe, and she was my born enemy. Javier's only crime was to look upon her with a longing I recognized too deeply.

I'd been given the option to take her head and end her life, or free my little bird to go back to her people while I slumbered deep in the mountains for a time of my father's choosing. I chose to free her because no matter how selfish I was, or how rare she had become, I chose her life over my desires. Living in a world where Avery didn't exist seemed like a world in which I wouldn't choose to live. I'd walked her to my father, handed her over, and walked away from my imp. I'd been told she wouldn't remember me or any time she'd spent within the hive, and I'd agreed to let her go so that she could live. Knowing that when I awoke from my slumber, she wouldn't remember me, and she'd be my enemy once more.

Mayhem woke me and told me that Avery was missing and our family was murdered before piling feeders at my feet. He told me everything he knew while I drained them one by one, knowing he had to be wrong about what had happened to our family. It had to be a trick they played on me, and yet I'd walked into my father's home to nothing but the ashes of those I'd loved. The scent of Avery's magic and betrayal was so thickly embedded in that tomb I knew I was just as guilty by saving her life which ended in a betrayal so dark and deadly that my family had paid the cost. She'd given me love, and then she'd destroyed it.

I felt her hatred in that place of death, the stench of darkness sent a chill up my spine. It hadn't been a simple act of revenge for leaving her; it was a slaughter done in a rage so dark and deadly that not even immortals had survived. She'd taken my family from me, and like a thief in the night, she walked away with her memories intact, and one by one, hives had been burned to the ground that no one had known about, no one except her. She murdered thousands of innocent vampires by the time she was finished, and I'd been too lost in my grief and blinded love to stop her.

"You're not fucking hearing me, Conner," Luca said, pulling me out of the memories and back to the current situation. "Fated mates were the shit of legends. It terrified anyone who thought they held the bond. It was forbidden even to whisper it when the world was new. Mating in such a way was deadly; it was an addiction that no one fucking wanted or understood. You had a connection on a level so deep that you knew what the other felt or needed before even they knew it. They didn't get a visible mark, because it was more than a true mating mark. It was a mark so embedded within them it marked their souls. That's called a fucking soulmate, in case you're not following me, asshole."

"What the fuck does it have to do with her?"

"She's your soulmate, Conner."

"What? No, I'd feel her."

"She died," he pointed out carefully. "She's been brought back more than once. Not by blood, Conner. Not by your essence, but by a powerful witch who chose to save her. It's in her aura, in her scent. Stop smelling her cunt and smell *her*. Something happened to Avery, and it may not be what she said it was, but something bad happened to her either way because I can sense trauma on her soul, and yet I can't see it. You say you want to breed her, but she said she couldn't, right? So why couldn't she? You said she was high on your blood when it mixed with hers. Soulmates can experience such a thing in our world. There's a fuck-ton of shit we don't know about them yet. Hell, there hasn't been one for decades that I am aware of. Avery wants you; she's unable to deny it, which is the same for you. Ever consider the fact that your addiction to her isn't an addiction at all? She committed genocide on the hive and yet you can't kill her, ever question why that is? Fuck, you *let* her go. You caught a fucking unicorn, and you released it into the wild instead of taking its head as a fucking trophy. Cheveron witches are the shit of myths, and you have one, naked in your bed, and you pissed it off. I don't know if I should pray or kneel at your fucking feet. Then there's the fact you want to keep her like she's a fucking pet. She's not a kitten; she's a fucking lion that will eat your fucking head the moment she can."

"She will pay for what she did, and I'm very aware of how unique she is. She's aware of it as well, and yet she chooses not to wield it, or use it. She isn't bound, and yet she hasn't lifted a single finger against me, although she thought to harm Amery because I was fucking her."

"You have her best friend in chains below. She's loyal, but how long will that last before she's had enough and fights back?"

"She could whisper a spell and slaughter us all, Luca. She either has no magic within her, or she doesn't want to hurt us."

"Wait, you don't know if she's a bomb waiting to go off, and you're waiting to see what she does?" he asked in a high-pitched tone as he pushed his fingers through his messy hair.

"How's the memory spell coming along?" I asked, ignoring the question.

"Answer the question, Conner. I have stood beside you through thick and thin, and you've never taken chances with our lives. You do what is needed for the hive, which is why I choose to stay at your side. You're a damn good King, but more than that, you're my best fucking friend. Tell me you're not doing this because you love her, tell me you won't let her murder us all because you're connected to her deeper than any-fucking-body should ever be!"

"I'd put her down before I let her hurt anyone here.

I taught that girl how to wield her magic; I know the taste of it by heart. I feel it before she even knows she's called it forth. How the fuck do you think I tracked her the moment she slipped out of the shadows? I felt her moving, felt the tang of magic that clung to her like a second skin, and knew the moment she stepped from the magic that prevented me from finding her. She's mine, she always has been, and she always will be. I have never looked upon another woman and not compared them to her, and they always fell short. I may be an asshole, but I know she is mine. She loved me; she still fucking does, because when she fucks me, I feel it there below the surface."

"Have you considered that maybe, just maybe, your father did as she said? If she is telling the truth, and you're unwilling to believe it…"

I swung around, leveling him with crimson eyes as my anger reared to life. "He wouldn't do that. He promised to keep her safe so I could go to my slumber and know she was safe from harm. He knew I loved her, which was why we were in the mess to fucking begin with. When I fell in love with that girl, it was a death sentence. They hunted her down, her own fucking people were trying to slaughter her any way they could. They intended to put her down like a rabid dog in the street because *she* loved *me*. My own people saw my affection for her as a weakness, and wanted to use her against her people."

"The King of the England Vampires had a Cheveron witch, alive and living within his hive for an entire year and no one ever saw her once during that time. Don't you think he made that shit known? It's in the books,

Con, your father put it there. You marked her for death by those covens by letting it be known he had one of them in his grasp, and not just one of them, but one of the most powerful bloodlines to ever rise from Hecate's womb in his fucking house. When you went to ground to slumber, she didn't. There are rumors within the witches of what happened, and they're not pretty. Do you think he actually took care of her for you? Think again. If I'm the King, and I have a fucking unicorn in a cage, I make it known. I let them know she's mine, and I'm keeping her. Pick up a fucking history book and read what he wrote. She's there, in those pages from his own hand, not another's. I'm not saying it to be a dick, I'm saying you left her, and only she and those who died know what happened there. Maybe the potion works, and you get answers, or maybe they're so fucking hidden within her that not even she remembers them. I hope you get your answers, and I also hope your mate doesn't murder us all when she is forced to relive the memories with you because that's how that shit works. Both of you have to remember it together, and if it is as bad as she says it was, pray that you don't also have to feel what she endured. There's a cost for the spell, it's a tit for fucking tat one, so maybe get drunk before you drink it."

"And if I have to murder her, you will be able to erase her from my mind?" I asked, needing it to happen. I'd considered it a thousand times before, erasing my imp from my mind, to forget she ever existed. I'd never gotten past thinking about it before I dismissed it.

"Yeah, I can do it, but if she is a part of you, you won't be able to ever erase the hole it will leave in you.

Soulmates are soul-deep, it's why crazy people pray to find them and sane people run from them."

"And the intoxication issue?" I countered, unsure I bought the whole soulmate shit. If she was, it explained a lot, but knowing that she may have betrayed me, and worse, hundreds of hives, and it left me in a precarious position that didn't sit well with me.

"It doesn't ever stop; it's a mixing of mates and their blood that has no explanation that would make sense to us. That's an entirely different type of magic. I don't envy you that shit. My advice, don't let that shit mix— or do, you said she was wild?"

"She was wild, but she was...different. It was like she looked through me, but didn't see me. Like she was stuck in another time or place, and I was the one thing holding her here. She wasn't my girl when she was on it; she was someone else."

"Like she was lost to memories?" he asked, even as he stepped away from me.

"My blood was saved to bring me back when the time came. It's what we use to awaken us from the slumber. I was awoken with *my* blood pulsing through *my* veins, no one else's."

"Diluted?" he countered.

"Don't you think I'd realize it if my blood was diluted?" I growled as I moved towards the bed, pushing the covers up where she'd dislodged them. Avery shivered as a moan left her lips and my cock twitched, even though she was in no shape to fix the blue balls she'd left me with.

"I think if the other half of your soul held it, and then was drained periodically, you'd never sense the difference. I think she's endured some kind of trauma to have that amulet on her throat. That's not a simple thing, there's ancient magic pulsing from it. That type of magic was used to create your kind, Conner. Born vampires aren't something that just snapped into existence. Somewhere in history, one of us brought one of you back and made life with it. That same magic brought your mate back from the trauma she endured. You need to prepare in case what it hides is something ugly, or something you can't fix. You loved her enough to let her go, and if she can't be tamed, you may need to do so again. I don't think you comprehend what being a soulmate entails. You won't kill her; you can't. You will watch that girl walk away from you because you won't want to live in a world where she doesn't exist. The thought alone makes you sick, doesn't it?"

"Get the fuck out, Luca."

"You got it, bro. I'm gone," he said, closing his bag before he headed to the door, stopping at the threshold to stare back at me before shaking his head and exiting the room.

He was dead right. I'd done it before, and though I may have loathed the idea, I'd never be the one to end her life, and I was the only one who could. She wasn't just mine by right; the spell that had brought her back from death's door had given me the power to end the life which I'd given to her. I'd stolen death from her, selfish prick that I had been, I couldn't let her join the thousands who had died to that sickness. Not when she'd tried to protect me, the monster who fed and terrorized her kind, from herself. Her gentleness called to my rough edges. Her shy smiles had appealed to the playboy I'd been back then. But her love, her love had been only hers to give, and she'd chosen to give it to me, blindly. Avery was the air I breathed, and the sun I could never stand within. She was the light to my darkness and the sun to my moon.

I'd never let the coven take her back, nor would I allow her to walk away from me. Not when she still kissed me as if she was starving and I was the only thing she craved. Life was cold and dead without her, and yet I sensed the changes within her. We couldn't ever go back to before I walked away, nor did I want to. I loved her then, and I loved her now, and I prayed she hadn't been planted to destroy us with every single fiber of my being. That was something not even a King could forgive or pardon.

CHAPTER ELEVEN

Avery

I studied Conner in the mirror as he dressed, noting the lack of his image and yet knew he stood in it not to see himself, but to watch me as he dressed. Today he'd slipped on jeans that hugged his ass nicely, with a dress shirt that exposed every contour of his chest like a second skin. I'd woken with the aftereffects of combining our blood as if I'd drunk too deeply the night before. I fingered the sheer white dress he had set on the bed and lifted my gaze, letting it linger on his strong frame. His head lifted, and I dropped my eyes to the bed.

"Look at me, imp," he said, turning to watch me. My eyes lifted, never meeting his as he moved closer to where I cradled my legs against my chest. "At me, Avery," he snapped angrily. "Not at my chest, not at my arms, look me in the fucking eyes."

I rose, kneeling on the bed in position before I spoke. "I'm your whore, Conner. Whores have one use, and we do not ever look into the eyes of our masters. I know where I belong, and I was taught what happens when little whores reach for that which is above them. I am fully aware of the pain that comes with disobedience. Can I give you pleasure or feed your hunger?"

"No, you can cut the fucking shit," he snarled. He watched me, studying my posture as I sat on my knees, eyes lowered in the pose his father had taught me through months of his so-called lessons. "I don't want some docile thing who won't even look me in the fucking eyes. I want the girl who feared no one or anything and took no shit, not even when she stood in a hive full of vampires who were born to be her enemy. I want that girl back, Avery."

My eyes lifted to his as something inside of me withered with his words. My heart ached, as if someone had reached into my chest and squeezed it. "You don't get her back, ever. She died the day you walked away from her and left her with those she'd refused to bow before. Do you have any idea how much they hated me? How much they craved to teach me that I was nothing, no better than a fucking pet? Don't ask me to be her, because I had to forget her and be what they wanted so that I could survive it."

"You keep saying that, and yet I knew them. I sacrificed everything to keep you safe. I gave up living for eternal slumber so that you could be free to live. He promised to erase me from your mind so that you could love again. That was what I sacrificed to keep you alive, to keep you safe from ever discovering what true pain was."

"No, Conner, he told you that so that he didn't

have to fight you. You left me right where he wanted me, and once you had been drained, your blood was used against me. You were the key to bringing me down because your father figured out that our blood combined together turned me into a dirty little thing that couldn't get enough of what he offered me. It's how I learned what our blood mixed together did to me. We'd always been careful, you and I, we didn't cross those lines. He shoved me to my limits, and sometimes, sometimes I would lose months in the darkness, and awaken less than I was before I'd been fed your blood. You see me as you knew me; I see a monster when I look in the mirror. I see what they made of me, and it isn't pretty. You want to know why I hid here, in the mountains. Because I wanted the solace it offered, the sanctuary that it awarded me. Mostly though, it reminded me of the peace I had with you before it was ripped away from me and I was turned into something less than human." I swallowed hard as he shook his head. "We never want to know that the world is a dark place, or that those we love are monsters. You want to know what turned me against the hive. Your blood running through my veins made me into their plaything, where they took turns doing whatever they wanted to do to me. Only, with you slumbering, you produced less and less, and I awoke a little more every single day. On the last day, when I had nothing left to lose, and I was brought out to be paraded before a hive of vampires as your father's mythical whore, I slaughtered every single fucking one of them with the evil, dark magic that begged me to let it out. I murdered every vampire who had ever touched me or hurt me. I bathed in their blood as I crawled out of that hell you'd left me to rot in. You want that girl back? Because she's an evil, heartless bitch who tasted blood and decided she fucking liked it."

"My father was the King, he was bound by his word," he argued.

"He was, but only to those who had heard him give it. Tell me, sweet prince, how many heard him give it to you?"

He ignored my question and dodged it with another mystery of his. "My blood was in a vault, next to where I slept."

"It was, but Mayhem had unlimited access to it too. He was told, by your father, that to protect you from the Spanish King, I had to die, and you had to enter eternal sleep, or we would both die. Your life or mine, Conner, who would *your* little brother have chosen to save?"

He stood up, pulling me from the bed as he grabbed the gown, slipping it over my head before he fixed it, roughly pulling my arms through the spaghetti strap sleeves, one by one. He didn't offer me shoes before he dragged me behind him at a hurried pace, forcing me to run to keep up with his long, angry strides. We burst into the main hall and screaming ripped from the far side of it, turning my blood to ice as Conner stalled in front of me, trying to shield me from what was happening.

"What the fuck, you were told to leave her alone. She is off-limits!" he shouted, and the room went silent around us.

"She was found outside, trying to escape her pretty cage. We tried to get her back into it, but she refused, and she cast on one of us," a deep voice said.

I pushed past Conner and stared in horror at Clara

who lay naked, bleeding on the floor from a multitude of bite marks. Everything inside of me tightened as my eyes lifted to the male who had mutilated her flesh, and magic unfurled, curling around me without warning as I sent it at him. Conner spun around, staring at me and then at the vampires around Clara who bellowed and screeched as pain took them to their knees. I smiled at the familiar sting of the magic as it slipped free from the tight hold I always had on it and then winced as something connected with my throat. More magic escaped, pushing and pushing until I gasped as something exploded from my lungs.

The magic faltered as my head connected against the floor with Conner above me. My eyes moved to his, holding them and his hand tightened on my throat as he crushed my larynx beneath his hold, assuming I'd whispered a spell.

"No, no more," he shouted as stars erupted in my vision. "I will not let you take anyone else from me, Avery!"

"You're killing her!" Laura's voice rang out through the crowd.

"She will never take more people from me," Conner whispered as anger burned in his eyes. He sat back, turning to stare at the vampires who were rising once more. "Luca, check them," he demanded as his eyes held mine.

He stood up, never looking away until he was at his full height. He stepped closer to his witch as I found Laura in the crowd, moving towards me while I held my throat, blood and spittle escaping as the air fought to come from my lungs and I struggled to get back to my feet, to check on Clara. She pointed at something behind me and I turned, watching as Addison tipped back a vial and then lunged forward, faster than my eyes could follow. My hands latched onto her shoulders as her fangs tore at my throat. I hissed as everything around me stopped.

Blood dripped from my lips as well as my throat and she pulled away from me, smiling with victory flashing in her eyes. My heart slowed as pain exploded from the wound in my throat. I turned slowly, searching for Laura and the protection she could give. I found Conner there, staring between his sister and me as my legs gave out and I fell onto my knees.

"Addison, what the fuck?" he snarled.

"I need to know what she did to our father!" she snapped as she stepped around my body as I crashed to the ground. Blood poured from the wound in my throat, coating the floor as it drenched my hair in the puddle I lay in. "Now we will know what happened. Now we can get... Ahh!" she screamed and fell to the floor, holding her stomach.

"Addison?" he growled and knelt beside her, moving his eyes between us as fear entered them. "Kill her," he whispered thickly. "Luca, take her down."

"It isn't her hurting your sister, my King. She took the potion I created for you. Avery isn't hurting her; she's reliving Avery's memories, and what is happening, it's because it happened *to* Avery."

Laura pushed her way to me, shoving Luca aside as she slipped through my blood on the floor beside me. Lifting my head, she peered down at the damage to my throat. Her lips moved, but nothing she said registered. I was being pulled back to hell with Addison. Pain ripped through my body, jackknifing my form as it began, tearing me apart from the inside out. Blood oozed from the open wound as blackness swallowed my vision. Laura screamed, cradling my face between her hands as her magic fought to keep me out of hell, where she knew I wouldn't return.

"The fuck is happening to her?" Conner demanded, his voice penetrating the blackness that offered me nothingness. His eyes watched me as if I'd give him the answer he sought. I wouldn't, and neither would she when she made it through the memories.

"You wanted answers; she will get them for you. I warned you, to take someone else's memories comes with a price. Your sister chose to pay it for you by stealing the potion I created and finished this morning."

"The fuck is happening to them if it's only memories?" Mayhem demanded as he knelt beside me, staring at the blood with open hunger, which shone in his expressive eyes. Worse, his eyes moved between Addison and me, and there was fear in them because he was aware of what I had endured, and now, everyone would know.

"Taste her, and you will die, brother," Conner seethed. "The next fucking person to make a move in this room dies."

"Fuck you and your obsession over this witch right now. You got bigger issues brewing, Conner."

"And what could be worse than what is fucking happening here?" he countered.

"There are witches outside," he muttered.

"Which coven has come?" Conner asked.

"All of them."

"Come again?" he demanded.

"There are over a thousand witches surrounding this mansion as we speak. The demand is easy enough to guess. They want their children freed from the school, and they want the witches you took from it back."

"Luca?" he asked as Laura smiled down at me while she held my neck closed.

"It would seem they've come at last to retrieve what you took from them. It's not many covens; it is only one coven and a handful of elders. It's just a really fucking large, very ancient, and very powerful coven, Conner."

"Prepare to defend the mansion," Conner said as he knelt, opening his wrist as he pushed it against my lips. "Close the day blinds, seal the door, and send word to Christian to seal the school and hold it at all costs. Seems they think to take you from me, imp."

I dropped my eyes while Addison began to flop across the floor, screaming as she was ripped apart from the pain I'd endured at her father's hands. He thought she'd tell him everything, but I'd considered that well before I'd allowed the amulet to be crafted, and not even his young witch could take my tale from me. Only I could give it to Conner, and in order to tell it and make him believe it, I'd have to show him the proof, which wasn't something I wanted to do. I lived with the knowledge of what I looked like before and after Grigori had destroyed me. I carried the shame of it so fucking deep that it had almost consumed me, and so together, Laura had helped me conceal it, and hide the ugliness of that shame within me with magic.

CHAPTER TWELVE

I sat in a cell, staring through the bars at where Conner watched Addison as she came back from the memories that had nearly taken me under their spell. However, I was so much stronger than any of them knew or suspected. She groaned as her eyes searched for me, her body going upright as she stood, and I watched her head shaking as her mouth opened, and only a moan escaped her lips.

"What did you see?" Conner asked, and she turned, mumbling gibberish as Luca watched the smile spreading over my lips. "What, you're not making any fucking sense, Addison."

"She can't tell you," Luca noted, his heavy stare filling with mirth. "I should have seen that one coming."

"Seen what coming?" Conner demanded.

"Your pretty little witch spelled her memories. No one can tell you what happened to her *but* her. Addison knows what she endured, but she can't speak of it."

"Then write it down!" he said, ordering a guard to bring him the paper and pen.

"She can't do that either. It won't leave her lips or her fingers. She's beneath Avery's spell, and was the moment she tried to steal her memories from her."

"Pretty and smart, where did you find such a creature, Conner? Was he in a pile of rubbish as well?" I asked, smiling, and Conner's eyes turned to me.

"You fucking knew we would do this?" he asked.

"I knew sooner or later you would come for me. I didn't know when or how it would happen, only that you would. I did know you though, and the lengths you would go through to learn what that piece of a whoring guttersnipe father of yours had done to me. Look at your sister and tell me, does she look happy? Does she look like she saw what you said would happen? She can't even look at me without crying. Now be a good boy and let me the fuck out of here before I let loose on your entire hive and bring it all down while you watch it happen."

"You think you can just walk out that front gate and live freely?" he countered as his eyes turned black. "You murdered hundreds of innocent lives by giving out the information to the locations of the hives I had personally taken you to visit. You have been hunted since the moment I rose from my sleep, until the moment rumors spread of your location. Right now there are hundreds of hives gearing up to come here, to kill the Cheveron witch who betrayed her vampire lover."

I blinked before a frown creased my brow. "I did nothing of the sort, Conner. I left that hive, which I freely admit to slaughtering, but I never helped anyone to find the other vampires. It took twenty years to fucking heal and allow the magic Laura cast on me to work. I didn't betray them; I couldn't have, considering everything I lost. Isn't that right, Addison?" I asked, and she bent over, throwing up blood onto the floor. "You shouldn't ever fuck with magic that you don't comprehend. You can't handle what I lived through, princess. Tell me, do you still love your sweet, gentle daddy now?" I laughed coldly, watching while she threw up again until she hiccupped and shook her head violently. "Me either, girl," I chuckled. "He was one twisted, sick puppy, wasn't he?"

I watched as she slid down the wall and pulled her knees up to her chest and began rocking to ease the memories from her mind. I almost felt bad for her, almost. I dropped to my knees and Conner looked between us, noting the shade of green his sister turned as she stared at me with wide, horrified eyes with tears of blood sliding down her face.

"It's true, isn't it?" he whispered hoarsely, staring at his sister, who in turn, stared at me with horrified revulsion as she saw me as I'd been in the memories. Conner looked at me with unease and pity.

"I don't want your pity, nor do I want you. What happened, and what you inadvertently allowed to happen to me took everything from me. I didn't just lose my family. I lost myself in that place, Conner. I lived because you took death away from me. At night, I'd pray for you to come into that room, but not to save me; to end it, to end *me*. To take away the immortality that you cursed me with. What I allowed Addison to see and feel was only the beginning of what I endured beneath your father's *protection*."

"I didn't know what happened, because I was too

busy trying to save your life. I killed the prince of the Spanish Vampires because he thought to take you from us. I slaughtered witches who hunted you because of the slight they thought you'd done by fucking a vampire. I murdered any vampire who thought to look upon you with lust or hatred. I fucking sheltered you from it all, and never let you know how much danger you were in because I didn't want you to live looking over your shoulder, wondering when they'd finally get to you."

"I would have been safer with them," I stated as I stood up, moving my hand as the clasp of the cell door exploded and tumbled to the floor, echoing through the room. "I am the granddaughter of Hecate, she who guards me from those who wish to harm me. I am the daughter of Ilsa Cheveron, who carried her mother's mark upon her flesh." I stopped in front of him and then winced as Addison wrapped her arms around me.

"I'm so sorry; I didn't know. We didn't know, Avery," she whispered as she looked up at me with bloody tears covering her face.

"Addison, I'm trying to be a badass here, and you're so ruining it," I hissed.

"You have to know that he had no idea, none of us did!" she hiccupped.

"Mayhem did, but him, I understood. I felt other magic that filled him, but also his need to protect me as best as he could, considering everything happening around us. He protected Conner, and I knew why he did it. The only reason he lives is because when he took his turn with me, it was to whisper into my ear that I was strong enough to survive it, and not to fuck me as everyone else did, but to survive until Conner could reach me and that when the time came, he'd tell Conner everything. Yet he couldn't, could he? I don't blame him, I mean, how *do* you tell your brother that you watched his mate being fucked by the hive repeatedly, and fed from until she died, only to be denied death because as long as he lived, she couldn't die. Or better yet, that she was chained in his father's room and used as his personal whore until he grew bored of her?"

"He doesn't deserve death," she pleaded.

"I have no intention of murdering Conner. I will stand trial by my peers, and if they are just, I will abide by their ruling. I will not, however, be caged anymore by any of your family," I said, pushing her away as I materialized in front of Conner, cupping his cheek. "Call your elder in, love. I'm not getting any younger, and I will leave within the hour one way or another."

"And if I say no?" he asked.

"You won't, because right now you're trying to imagine how much I endured, and you know the depravity of the hive when they took their enemy's bride to that deep, dark hole. I *wish* I had been someone's bride because it makes what I had to endure look fucking fun. You will let me go because of it, and because I know what you will ask of me, and when you do, you will never be able to forget it."

"You're my mate, Avery," he whispered as his hand cupped my cheek.

"No, I wasn't just your mate. I was your *soul*mate. Soulmates are tricky things, Conner. I couldn't tell you what you should have felt or known from the beginning. That's why your blood ignites me, drugging my soul until the only thing I know or want is you. I learned that lesson without you, and now I know why sane people avoid that bond at all cost. It destroys you; it rips you apart when they abandon you. Torture I could have endured, being shared with the hive and used any way they wished to use me, fine, being used as a feeder for your brothers and father, whatever. Losing *you*, well, that broke me more than any of them could have ever broken me. I learned to live without you while still feeling this bond, and you can do it too."

"You will stand trial against your peers, Avery." His hand dropped from me as he watched me through pain-filled eyes. "You will be judged at their hand, and then you can walk away if you so choose. If they choose death, you will never know it. I hold that card in my hand, and I won't live in a world where you don't exist, even if I cannot hold you or touch you. I will send for you when they're ready to convene your sentence."

CHAPTER THIRTEEN

I could hear them outside the antechamber as they argued and fought about what the charges would be. Technically, I'd never broken any law or any covenant that could be proven. My secrets were hidden within me, and only one person knew them, and she would die before she ever spoke a word of it, by choice on a freely given oath. Our coven laws forbid her from betraying a secret told in the shadows, under the sanctuary of sisterhood, and I'd been sure that an oath had been given.

To Conner, I'd promised love, but I'd never broken any laws since he'd never asked me to betray the covenant or my vow to my coven. Even though they'd perished long ago, I'd honored the one I made to them still. Laura was pissed, her oath to me was being questioned, and our time teaching the students at the academy, everything we'd ever done to help benefit the coven was now compromised because my past was clashing with the present.

The door cracked open, and I spun around slowly,

assuming it would be either Laura or Clara, but instead, Conner stood there. His tall frame blocked out the light, shadowing his features as I dropped my eyes from his and crinkled my brow.

"What do you want?" I asked hesitantly when all he continued to do was look at me expectantly. I fidgeted with my hands, sensing his need to speak, and yet he didn't.

"I'll be the one to bring you before the witches and my elder in residence. I came to tell you of other factors that will be out of my hands during this time. The Anderson King and his son have reached us and will sit in judgment of you, but have declined to speak of it or hold you into account for your actions. There are more coming to the Inland Northwest to capture you for your crimes on their hives. I can't stop it this time, Avery. I need you to ask me for sanctuary, and I will give it. Do you understand me?"

"I don't need you to save me, Conner. I can save myself now. The Anderson King is weak and has an infliction of the blood. He will die within the year, and his son, Heron will take his crown. I know Heron, and I have helped him take the crown through any means necessary to stop his father's murderous reign. Someone had to do it, and none of you seemed to be bothered that he slaughtered hundreds of innocent babes in his incurable hunger. Do you think I have not planted pieces into play? You taught me always to stack the board before I ever started to play the game. The other hives, well, they can either get on my side or stand in my way. I don't think they will like the latter option or the consequences. You think of me as a child, and I assure you, I am not. I have learned the ways of the world, thanks to you. I have learned many things at the hands of my enemies, and I assure you, sweet princeling, you and your kind are my fucking enemy. You and I may have been written in the stars, but even stars burn out."

"There you are, my fiery Queen of the Witches," he chuckled as he nodded, even though his eyes filled with sadness while I watched him. "I told you that one day, you could rule them all and you laughed and told me that without a King, a Queen is nothing. I argued it against you, knowing that one day, you'd become a Queen regardless of who stood beside you. Did you never wonder why I never asked you to betray your people, a people you would one day rule?"

I shook my head, wondering where this was coming from now, of all times. "No, I was a misguided girl who thought you loved her. I thought you hung the moon and then placed the stars into the darkness to keep me from being scared of the monsters, when the entire time, I was standing in their midst just waiting for them to consume me."

He flinched from my words, and I smiled sadly, knowing the barb had hit home. When he spoke again, his tone was sure, confident. "I knew I was standing beside the Queen of the Witches, and should she ever choose to rise, I wanted her on my side. Avery, I have loved you since before you were ready to be loved. I never stopped loving you or looking for you in a crowded room. You chose to make me King, knowing that it would force me to ascend to my throne. I thought you wanted me to be King, to argue the laws of our people. That was my first thought when I raced home and found everyone dead. I waited in that burned-out shell of my family's home for you, but you never came back to me, and I went to a very dark place because my soul was fractured. I blamed you because you weren't there, and I needed you, and I could taste the darkness of your magic, and it hurt to know you murdered my family because there was no denying the truth that they had died by your hand. You just disappeared, as if you'd never even existed. There was nothing of yours left in your rooms or in mine. The items that I'd hidden to remember you by, they were gone from the tombs where I'd kept them. The only thing that lingered after you vanished was your scent, the tang of your magic, and the whisper of peonies in spring," he said as his hand lifted, cupping my cheek as he slowly placed his forehead against mine before he gently kissed it. "I left you there to save you, to keep you from ever knowing true pain. I failed you, and for that, I don't expect you ever to forgive me."

"Good," I uttered hoarsely as I pulled away from his touch. "Because I don't, nor do I care to linger within a hive. Take me to my trial, Conner. I'm sure they're wondering what is keeping us."

He pulled back, dropping his hand as he stared down at me. "As you wish, imp."

I followed him down a long, winding hallway before we entered the grand hall. It was larger than the throne room where he'd taken me before. This one had a raised dais, with one throne carved with the moon, and the other engraved with a sun and moon, the sign of witchcraft that he used to whittle for me out of wood proudly sitting on the front of them. My steps faltered and stalled my progression, studying the initials that sat in the moon and sun. My eyes moved to his back, watching as he waited, knowing just what had stalled my steps.

"I had it made long before I lost you," he whispered, barely loud enough to make out through the crowd that was now murmuring in confusion about our sudden pause. I stared at him, unable to pull my gaze from where he waited for me to begin walking again.

I'd always believed that he'd known what had befallen me. I'd waited for him to come, to save me, and when he never did, I'd given up on us; on *him* and any future we may have had or planned. His words replayed through my mind, his slumbering to save me, as if we'd been some fucking fairytale and he'd been selfless, when nothing in our world was ever so fantastical. It was brutal, chaotic, horrifyingly real shit that ripped you apart and spat out something that barely resembled what you'd been. I knew because I'd lost who I had been in order to survive the horror of what had been done to me.

I took a step forward, watching as Conner lowered his head and began to move once more. I followed him pensively, lost in my thoughts as we moved to where chairs had been set behind a large oak table that spread across the room. It was a tribune, created of those who stood witness in judgment for major crimes against the covenant that was now in place. The only law I'd ever broken was to love my enemy in a time when it was forbidden, and I paid for it in blood. I stopped beside Laura, who nodded to me with reassurance.

"Avery Ilsa Cheveron, you stand accused of treason

against your coven. You are to be judged by a tribunal of your peers. How do you plead?" Roger, Flora's father, asked.

Conner swore as Mayhem moved to stop him from rising from his chair, where he sat beside the vampire elder who watched me through bright, ice-blue eyes. His hair was jet-black and shone beneath the bright lights that bathed his bronzed flesh in a radiant glow. Arthur MacDougall had been born before Ireland was ever invaded by the fairies and was one of the very few vampires old enough to withstand sunlight. Those eyes of his though, they looked through me, as if he could see the real me.

"Not guilty," I said, turning as I narrowed my eyes on Roger, noting the sweat that dripped from his temples. He didn't enjoy being here, in a room filled with creatures that would just as soon see him skinned alive. I noted the aura that coated his flesh and swallowed hard, remembering another time I'd seen it long ago.

I turned to check Laura, watching as her eyes left his to hold mine. She'd sensed it too; the oily taint of dark magic was coating his flesh and moving between him and the other witches. My heart began to hammer against my ribs, as if it would break free from the cage that held it. Laura's hand touched my shoulder, giving me reassurance that I wasn't alone.

"She isn't guilty of treason against her coven. Her coven died to the plague, and she did what she had to do to survive," Conner said, drawing my gaze to his. "You were brought here to protect her from our judgment, and yet you think to condemn her for treason, which is punishable by death?"

"It is none of your concern," Roger argued vehemently.

"Isn't it? You came here to request her release from us, when she is in our possession, Roger. Now, let us begin again," Arthur said while his eyes studied me carefully. "Avery, you are charged with loving a vampire, one who sacrificed himself to protect you. His family then paid the price."

"She swore she gave no vow or oath to them or her lover." Roger looked troubled and his eyes continued to bug out as he spoke, like he was choking on something and couldn't get it out.

"Still, we will hear her story and know what happened to his family as is his right as King. I must remind you, Roger, Conner helped write the covenant that we now follow. He also holds her in his possession and has agreed to this tribune to decide her fate even though he didn't have to allow it by right of possession. Should you wish to charge her for treason, do it on your own time," Arthur hissed, smirking at me before winking.

"She will stand trial here, before the lover she chose over her dying mother," Selena growled, shocking me.

I eyed her with a look of disbelief as her dull eyes stared through me. Her aura was black as well, turning darker than the shadows that filled her eyes. I swallowed hard, fighting against nausea that swirled through me. Again, Laura touched my shoulder, bringing me back to the present and away from the nightmares that clawed from the depths in which I'd banished them.

Luca approached me slowly, his hand lifted, offering a concoction that was held in an amazonite flask. He stretched his hand as he spoke low, clear, and confidently. "In this flask is a truth serum, from this point until the end of your trial, you will only be able to speak the truth, Avery."

I stared at his outstretched hand, knowing that once I took it, Conner would know everything. He'd be able to ask me anything, and I'd be unable to lie to withhold the horrid details of what had happened to me. I swung my gaze to him, watching as his eyes captured mine and then lowered, unable to hold it.

"I understand," I whispered thickly.

I knew once he learned of my past, he would never look at me in the same way. Once he saw the truth of what I'd endured, he'd never want me as he had before I'd been ruined. I took the flask and tipped it back, praying it wasn't instant. Laura slipped her hand into mine, giving me her strength as the spell burned through me. My mind cleared as it settled, slipping through my mind to my tongue, and then wrapping around my heart. I looked away from Conner, and back to Luca, who frowned as lights burst behind my eyes.

"She's ready to be questioned, my King," he announced, and yet there was no resentment in his tone, only worry for what they would find in my story. Conner would lose what respect he'd known for his father and brothers, and worse, he'd hate me by the end of this tale, more than when he thought I murdered them out of spite.

CHAPTER
FOURTEEN

I waited, staring at the floor as Conner watched me fidgeting where I stood, barefooted and dressed in the silky white gown he'd handed me hours ago, now red from my blood where his sister had attacked my throat. My face was covered in blood, my hair a sticky mess, and I'd never asked them for a washcloth, which I now regretted. He cleared his throat, and I lifted my eyes to hold his, somehow keeping the fear from showing in them.

"Was it ever real?" he asked, and I sucked my lip between my teeth, narrowing my green eyes on his pretty violet ones.

"Was what real, Conner?" I asked, needing him to clarify his question.

"Did you ever love me?"

"With everything I had and everything I was, I loved you," I answered softly, my hands moving together as my finger pinched between my thumb and pointer finger to keep me grounded.

"Do you still love me?" he countered.

"I do, and I always will. I think you should focus on what you need to know, instead of what you want to know, King Halverson."

"You will answer whatever I ask you," he replied in a dangerously dark tone. "I left you in the care of my father, a man who helped to keep you safe and protected while you were with us, and you killed him."

He waited, and I smiled sadly, watching his eyes while they narrowed on me as he continued to wait for the answer to his statement. I wanted to warn him, to tell him that this wasn't something he needed, or wanted to know, no matter how much he thought he did.

"Conner, that wasn't a question."

"How many men of the hive did you lay down with willingly?" he amended.

"All of them, and some of the women as well," I replied as the hold on my flesh turned painful.

"You said they raped you, and yet you say under a truth spell that you did so willingly. It can't be both."

"It was rape before they discovered that our blood made me willing to do whatever they wanted from me. At first, I was the entertainment. I was beaten, raped, and the King's personal feeder. I fought him the best I could with my hands bound, my body beaten. For an entire month, I was left tied to the pole where they took the traitors' brides and murdered them. He raped me whenever he felt the urge to show the hive, I was his. He made me offers to turn against the witches, and he'd take me down from the pole and only keep me in his room to use. No one would be able to see him defile me anymore, but I refused. I refused to give the King who had become like a father to me an oath of fidelity.

"One month in something happened, something I still don't understand, and yet I felt him ripping me open. When I awoke, it was with your blood pulsing through me, enough that the pain lessened a bit, but what I found was horrifying. He'd ripped me from sternum to pelvis, allowing his doctor to crudely sew me back together. Those weren't the only scars I had; there were many more. I was put back on the pole, and it was then I was given a traitor's death, but once again, I couldn't die because you merely slumbered within the great mountains. I bled out many times, and each time, I was given more blood. Your father once again offered me a chance to serve him, and once more, I refused. I was beaten until I could no longer speak or move, and it was then that he forced your blood down my throat. What happened after that, changed everything.

"I became their willing whore, one who craved what they did to me. I couldn't get enough. I was put into a room, and those who earned it or pleased their King were allowed to do whatever they wished to me. Every man you hurt, every vampire who had been denied a taste or a touch of me when I had been yours, well, they showed me what good little whores get, and then they beat me for fun. I took many at once, or whatever they wanted me to take. Women used me, and what they used on me were crude things, and under the influence of your blood, I didn't beg them to stop. I would wake up covered in my blood, torn apart day after day, only to be given your blood to heal me and do it all over again.

"After some time had passed, your father decided he wished to teach me my place and refused me the blood that would have eased my pain. I learned to service my master on my knees at his feet or in the darkest place within his keep. Sometimes, I was chained there, left for weeks to rot until he remembered I existed in that dark room where he kept me. Your brothers, your oh so sweet brothers, enjoyed me together. They were a special breed, using every part of me that could fit them; sometimes they just tortured me to see how far it could go before I succumbed to death, only to come back from it again. Your father watched us often, enjoying the screams of pain that escaped my lungs when they fed from me, or put more into me than I could take at once. I endured, and I survived because I couldn't do anything else. I was immortally hexed, and no matter how much my soul died, my body refused to allow it to escape the endless pain. Is this what you want to know? That I played the whore and I sucked their cocks to survive. That I did everyone in that hive who wanted to fuck me? Is that what you want, or did you want to know that their depravity was real?"

He didn't say anything, nor would he look at me as tears ran down my cheeks to drop as crystals upon the floor. When he finally did look at me, it was with anger burning in his eyes. The bluish-purple fire that locked with mine told me that even with his witch's spell pulsing through my system, he didn't believe what I said.

"You're not vampire, Avery Cheveron. You carry no scars to prove your words. I've seen every inch of your flesh, and you have only a few scars to mar that utterly perfect body of yours. You're as beautiful as you were the day I made you into a woman. So, tell me, witch, how is that possible?"

I stared at him with mirth and anger driving me deeper into the pits of despair that I fought against. The depression Laura had dragged me out of, the anxiety that I'd never be whole again after what they'd done to me, and it all collided together into a force that almost made me drop to my knees.

"Yes, show us how that is possible," Roger agreed. I turned my stare towards him, frowning as he looked at me expectantly. "I said, show us your proof. You are, after all, a witch and not a vampire, correct?"

"I am, and I will show you," I said even as Laura began to argue. I paused, turning to look at her panicked face. "It's the only way they will believe me."

"Who cares if they do? I don't. This is bullshit; you've suffered enough at their hands. It took twenty years for me to bring you back from what those sick assholes did to you. Twenty years of not knowing if what I did was enough to fix the damage they did to you. You owe these assholes nothing! You don't owe them shit, Avery. Don't do this."

"I remember how hard you fought to bring me back, but unless they see it, it won't be real. It will only be words I say, so let them see what they have done to me," I said as I reached down, lifting the hem of the gown to reveal my stomach and naked breasts. I handed it to her, turning to look at Conner, who narrowed his eyes on me, not liking that I'd stripped before a room full of men and women, but this was the only way I could prove what had been done to me. I took in the lust of his heady stare, the way he gazed on me as if I was some mythical creature that had been crafted in the stars purely for him. It was the last time I'd see it, the last time he'd be able to see what he wanted to and not the monster beneath the glamour of the magic I wore to hide it. My hands shook as I reached for my necklace, turning my back to him as I faced the crowd who watched us silently.

I lifted my eyes to the crowd and whispered a spell as my fingers continued to touch the amulet, and then there was the familiar weight of it being removed. My hand stretched out with the trinket in it, and Laura stared down at it with tears swimming in her eyes as she accepted the amulet and stepped back from me. The familiar bite of pain ripped through me as the crowd watched my transformation. Gasps sounded around me, even Conner uttered beneath his breath as he took in my mutilated back where I'd been whipped until death over and over again, with Grigori rubbing salt into the wound to keep it from healing, and to be sure I carried the scar to remind me I'd been bad to refuse him. I exhaled and turned to face the man who held my soul, and yet I wouldn't look at him through the haze that covered my eyes. They were white, sightless eyes that had yet to fully heal from the burns that had taken them from me, removing my sight. On my forehead was his family seal, written beneath it crudely was my status, *Whore*. On my cheeks were twin tattoos; both were upside down crosses to signify evil. Unlike the scar written above them, black ink had been used to place them, mixed with salt to ensure they didn't fade or disappear over time. My breasts had been removed since, of course, they'd been Conner's favorite part of my body. A scar went from below the white panties I wore to my sternum. Hundreds of bite marks covered my body, including my neck, waist, stomach, and inner thighs. My fingers had been removed, and not a single inch of me had been left untouched by their brutality. The scar on my neck was long and jagged, thick with an entire year of abuse that had left it damaged in case what else they took from me grew back so that I couldn't whisper a spell.

"They did this to you?" he whispered barely loud enough to be heard.

"She cannot answer you. They took her tongue to be sure she couldn't whisper her magic. They removed her points to be sure she was helpless against them. Avery killed your hive with dark magic, not light. She had no way to wield it, no tongue to say words of magic, and no points to conduct it. When she killed them, it was out of sheer desperation to survive. I found her dying over and over again in the gutter where she bled out from whoever had decided to rip her throat out. I do believe where she went to die again was in the same place you'd found her before. Only she couldn't die. I took her to my coven, and together, we started to work on a way to save her life. Twenty years from the day I had discovered her mutilated body, the spell to hide her damage came to us, and I used it. I spent many years with her, trying to convince her that they'd deserved what she had done. Still, she defended you against me. You did this to her, and while she may forgive your kind for doing this to her, I don't."

Laura turned, pulling me closer to her as she placed the necklace back onto my throat and whispered the words that I couldn't. I allowed her to help me dress, unable to pick up the gown she'd dropped or move from where I balanced without my toes to steady me. No noise filled the assembly of creatures that had stared at me aghast, horrified by the sight of my mutilated body. I didn't blame them; the first time I'd taken in what I looked like, I'd moaned, unable to even scream at the monster who had gazed through sightless eyes into that blurry silver mirror. That day, it haunted me every time I passed a mirror, and so I'd had every one of them taken out of the academy to be sure those memories remained buried. I'd thrown myself into helping the lost and abused, the misfortunate souls that had ever suffered or lost a part of them.

I moaned as I tried to make words come out, and yet nothing did. I turned back to the council, watching Roger as he blanched, now fully aware of what lay beneath the veneer I wore to hide the scars and the abuse I'd survived. I swallowed hard several times as I let the magic wash through me while I used my phantom fingers to fix the gown I wore. The good thing about the spell was that I felt real, and each part that it brought back, like fingers, had feeling even if it was only phantom-like feeling.

"You have paid more than anyone should ever have to," Arthur said without emotion marring his words. "I will ask no price of blood, nor debt to be paid from you. Conner, do you agree?" he asked, turning to look at Conner, who had yet to speak.

"I agree, she has suffered enough from us and shall be free from any judgment or further punishment."

"We will vote to see if she will be tried for treason," Roger announced, and one by one, the witches voiced their opinion, until only one remained. Harley smiled, her pristine white teeth too white, her eyes too blue and filled with victory as she whispered the final "Aye." I smiled as I watched her, noting the discoloration of her lips, and the lines that pulled her face too tightly from her hair.

"I will not stand accused of treason for crimes that you make up. I committed no treason against any witch or coven. I didn't order or help in the deaths of the vampire hives either. There was only one other witch who knew of their location at that time, isn't that right, Hemlock?" I asked and smirked as he stared at me with smiling eyes. I could feel him, the vileness of his ill-magic as it filled the other witches around him, driving a single thought into their minds. His magic had helped to save me so long ago, and yet Conner had trusted his motives and murdered him to keep me safe. Apparently, Hemlock had taken steps in case such a thing ever occurred. It helped a lot of other things that had happened make sense. Like my overwhelming need to breed back then, but I'd been naïve and untrained during that time. It wasn't the case now.

"Avery, I killed Hemlock once he'd figured out the spell to make you immortal." Conner's tone didn't carry a lie; in fact, he'd probably assumed he had managed to kill the witch. But we were nothing, if not for survivors.

"The same witch who made me immortal? The same one who bound my soul to yours and gave you the power to determine if I lived or died? He took the same spell and used it; of that you can be sure. Our mantra is to survive, and so he has."

"It's a woman," Arthur injected into the conversation as he stared at the body Hemlock projected. My guess was that poor Harley was somewhere dead with her throat slit.

I struck before they could stop me, letting the power ooze from my pores as I erupted into action, landing on Hemlock's lap. I leaned over, whispering a spell to show me what truly lay beneath the spell he wore. Dull brown eyes held mine while graying hair spread over his head. His flesh contorted, losing the delicate features for more masculine ones. I leaned in closer, placing my lips against his as I inhaled his magic, draining him of everything that he had within him, leaving him a mere mortal as I sat up onto the table with him between my legs, gasping for air.

"You fucking bitch! You and your whore swine took everything from me. *Everything!* Then, after I'd done what he had asked, and it was my turn to become immortal like you, he murdered me. But I knew he would, and I took steps to ensure that I survived at all cost. Neither of you ever felt my touch of magic as I made you breed so that I could have a child with your bloodlines to rule the world! Then, I made him murder the Prince of the Spanish Vampires, and as he lay slumbering, I watched them mutilate his perfect mate as he slept; his fucking soulmate was tortured and ripped apart as he lay helpless in his slumber, never knowing what happened to you because my magic shielded him from your pain. You think I didn't enjoy that sweet flesh of yours too? Grigori allowed me between these perfect thighs as much as I wanted, and oh, did I want it. You never even knew it was me who fucked you, taking you over and over as you begged for death. I had them all under my spell, none ever felt it either. I am a better witch than you will ever be, Cheveron. I even helped them hide the monstrous little bitch you carried in your poisonous womb. Not even Mayhem realized he was beneath my spell the entire time he brought you Conner's blood, or if he did, he was spelled never to tell him the truth. You never even knew you had done it, created a life with your precious prince. You had no idea that Grigori had heard its heart beating and ripped you apart to remove his granddaughter from your worthless, dying womb because I helped him drug you and keep you unaware of what happened other than the pain. That, I let you feel; every tear of your flesh, every bite of his fangs was like being torn open again, wasn't it? I helped them keep you alive, revealing to them the drug his blood would become to you. I am the witch who helped put your prince to sleep at his father's request, drugging his slumber so that he never felt your pain or your arousal as you played the perfect whore. I took from you both, as you took from me. I had planned to bring you to him once you'd endured a few centuries of torture and there was nothing left of you but your pretty holes, but you murdered them and ruined my plans."

I swallowed hard at his words, disbelief sweeping through me, and yet I didn't buy it. Had I created a life with Conner, I'd have felt it. I'd have known it because I'd craved it; I'd craved it as much as I had the need to love Conner. I opened my mouth to call him out on it as something pushed through his chest, reaching out toward me, holding a rotting organ. I lifted my gaze, locking eyes with Conner's as he stared at me, unseeingly. His hand withdrew through the gaping hole in Hemlock's chest as the man crumpled face-first into my lap. I gagged on a vileness that slithered up my spine and forced a violent shudder to move through me. It felt as if something had been unleashed upon Hemlock's death, and I whimpered as Conner hissed; he had felt it as well. I shoved his corpse away, standing to face Conner.

"Mayhem, take his body to the tunnel and have bricks placed around it. See that he cannot escape and then you and me, we will have a talk. This tribunal is over. My hive will stand beside Avery, and we will go to war against any who think to harm her. My father's death at her hands was justified. I will not seek retribution for what was done to them," he stepped back as my power continued to unfurl. "Take your coven and leave, Roger."

"That is not my coven outside these walls," he snorted as he stood up, ready to run.

"No, then who do they belong to?" Conner snapped.

"Me," I whispered as I watched him looking anywhere but at me.

"You were forbidden to form a coven!" Roger hissed.

"I was, but I do not go by your laws or any laws that have been made. I am a Cheveron witch, Roger. I was born to be your Queen, be glad I do not care to ascend to my rightful position. Witches like you would be removed from the covenant, along with the council. Now leave," I stated.

"He still has control of the school!" he argued.

I lifted my gaze to where Conner stared at something over my shoulder. "Is that true?" I demanded.

"The students have been released as of this morning. It is yours to return to."

"There will be no more witches sent to you for training! You are an abomination!"

I smiled as I swayed my hips and walked towards him. Scenting his fear as I approached, I leaned over and gently brushed my lips against his as my magic held him prisoner. I consumed his magic; every single ounce of power he held vanished to enter me, a more powerful host. "And you're fucking mortal, so who has more issues now? You, who now has no magic and must leave the coven, or me, who took in the unwanted, the damaged and broken things that no one wanted to see? I could own the world, should I ever choose to rule it. Anyone else want to poke jokes or talk shit before I go home?" I waited, turning to look at Conner, who dropped his eyes to the floor, refusing to look at me. "What's the matter, love? Am I not all you wished for? Didn't your daddy make me pretty enough for you? I guess he was right after all: you'd never want me knowing he had tainted my flesh and took away my beauty. Pity, I guess some things are just written upon burning stars that die out and leave even fate in despair."

Turning, I found Laura watching me carefully, knowing I felt pain at his rejection. I nodded to her before searching the room for Clara, who stepped forward, healed and physically whole again from what the vampires had done to her. Once she was beside Laura and me, we left, not bothering to say another word to the witches or vampires as they watched us slip through their ranks and walk out of their lives.

CHAPTER FIFTEEN

Six months later

I watched bad reality television in the main room of the academy, alone. I'd spent weeks in solitude, needing to once again bury the nightmares that plagued me. Now, getting Conner out of my system again, that would take centuries to achieve. I was covered in popcorn and butter when Laura entered the room, huffing and out of breath as she slid to a halt in front of me. Lucky for me, Clara was still healing and left me alone. While she carried no scars from her trauma, her mind still felt everything that had happened to her. She was like me now, broken, but learning to live with the pain she'd endured. That took time to accept, time to learn how to live with the memories. She was coming around, but she hardly left the basement of the academy or her rooms. Laura, on the other hand, the bitch had no pity for us or a shut-off switch, but that was one of the reasons I loved her sassy, snarky, take-no-shit ass.

"Get up," she demanded. "You have got to come see

this!"

I eyed her as I popped another delicious kernel into my mouth and crunched it. My eyes dropped back to the television as one of the girls slapped the male she'd been shacking up with, only to learn he'd done the same thing to the other girl in the house. I started to toss another kernel of buttery goodness into my mouth as Laura grabbed the tub and threw it into the growing mess around me.

"Conner was here," she seethed. "It had to be him; he's the only one with enough balls to have done this shit while we were sleeping."

"We don't say that name here," I grumbled as I looked down at the couch, finding a fallen piece of popcorn that I picked up and ate as she scrunched up her nose in disgust.

"Get your ass up, oh Queen of the Sofa, and come outside."

"I do make this sofa look hot, don't I?" I muttered beneath my breath as I stood up, dusting off the kernels with butter coating my fingers. "What is so important that you're disturbing my television time?"

"Come with me," she said and waved her arm one way as she started in the other direction. "I'm over this pity party, and I'm also over you allowing Clara to hide away in her rooms. You know she needs to be out of it, and yet you don't force it. Probably because you seem to be hiding from reality as well," she huffed.

"Which way am I going?" I asked as I held my fingers up, pointing to each exit. "Clara is learning a new normal, and that shit takes time. Would you decide which way we are going? I can do many things, but cloning myself isn't one of them, *yet*." I tapped my foot impatiently as I sniffed the air. "What is that smell?"

"You, *you* are that smell, Avery. You've been moping about for six months now. No one has the balls to stand up to the covenant, nor do they think you're sane anymore. You ate Roger's magic, and you did it in full view of other witches. Do you know how dangerous that is, or how deadly it could be to those who have chosen to follow you? Remember when we discussed the whole *you're not normal* spiel, and that if they knew, they'd move against us. Remember that?"

"What century did we have that argument?" I asked as I scratched my head, staring at her before bringing my fingers down to look at the butter that coated them. Okay, so maybe I should shower. "What time is it?"

"It's nighttime; you know, when your undead King is out about and roaming the woods. Now follow me, then you can shower and do something with…" she paused, then indicated all of me. "Do something with *that*."

"You don't know what I feel right now," I uttered as I wiped my hands on my sweats.

"That you feel like you can't fucking breathe without him? That it feels like your heart is being ripped out through your chest, and everything inside of you wants to lie down and die? No, I have no idea what it feels like. Love is shit, it is hard, and it is ugly and maybe, just fucking maybe, it's the universe's biggest joke that it plays on us. We will figure a way out of it. We have worked miracles together, Avery. We have survived time and time again through everything this world has thrown at us. One man, who can't even look at you anymore, isn't a challenge. He's a fucking problem and those we know how to handle."

"I don't want him handled; I want to forget him. I want to forget the way he can't look at me…" I paused when we reached the roof and a glow lit up the meadow. Slowly, I walked to the edge of the building, staring down at the glowing peonies that had been planted the entire length of the field.

"I was out here thirty minutes ago, and this field was empty. They're as far as you can see all around the building. Worse yet, he's out there, watching us."

"He is," I said as I stepped back, feeling the pull to him. "This makes no sense. Why plant flowers that I love unless it is to taunt me? Do you think he plans to fight me?" I asked, sucking my bottom lip between my teeth as I considered what this meant.

"Normally, when a guy wants to fight you, he doesn't plant an entire field of glowing flowers as a challenge or warning?" She shrugged. "Just saying, that doesn't scream fight club."

"Peonies, they're peonies that have been painted to shine beneath the moon's iridescent rays. It's the flower I *used* to love. He'd pick them for me, and I'd place them into my bath, and then I'd bathe as he watched me from the shadows. It left me vulnerable and drove him mad with longing since, at that time, we hadn't slept together."

"You guys have some serious issues," she replied as she leaned over, staring at the miles of flowers that surrounded us.

I lifted my gaze, sensing him in the shadows and pinpointing his location before I took another step backward. I knew better than to be outside at dusk, and yet it was past midnight, and he was at his strongest when the moon reached its zenith in the sky.

"Avery," his voice wafted to us, and I turned, escaping to the lighted staircase as my heart shattered again. "I need to see you. We need to talk without an audience around us."

I slid into the staircase and waited for Laura, who slowly made her way to me and closed the door behind us. She sat beside me as I lifted tear-filled eyes to hers. I couldn't do this again, because I'd wanted him. I'd never stopped wanting him; I'd just learned how to live without him. He was a part of me, and yet he couldn't even bring himself to look at me now, after seeing what lay beneath the magic I wore.

"You're stronger than you think. You're braver than you know you are, and your butt is rocking in those sweatpants, even the butter looks great on you," she uttered as she leaned forward, grasping my hand and pushing a hint of magic towards me in reassurance that I wasn't alone, and that this, too, would pass.

Every night at dusk, more flowers would appear. I'd taken to cutting them down when the sun rose, and every night, he and his hive replanted them. Three months passed with them doing it. Every night, he'd wait for me to come to the roof, to expose myself to the night, and every night, I'd stand in the staircase, feeling him right outside the door, waiting for me to come to him. One night, my hand touched the door, and I knew the moment his hand mirrored my action. Yanking it back, I leaned closer, listening to him breathing as he waited for me to come out.

"You can't hide forever," he said after time had passed in silence as we sat there, just feeling each other from a distance. "I need to see you; to know you're alright."

"I'm fine."

"You're not fine; you will never be fine again after what my family did to you. I won't be either. You were mine to keep safe. I agreed to my sentence because it allowed you to move on. It allowed you to go free and forget about me. I would have found you again, but for you, it wouldn't be as it had been. You wouldn't have remembered me. My father promised to keep you alive and make sure nothing happened to you. He wrecked you, abused you, and tortured you after giving me his word. He gave me his word as King to our hive and London. He promised me, as my father, that nothing would befall you, and that he would ensure you were safe from harm."

I sat in silence, listening to him breathing as he waited for me to reply. My head leaned against the door, and I felt his touch through it, the touching of souls that only soulmates shared. I craved it; I craved him. I stood up, dusting off my hands and knees before I left the staircase and took shelter in my room. That night, I dreamt of him before our world had been ripped apart, and when I'd loved him more than I had ever loved myself.

CHAPTER SIXTEEN

I stood in the meadow, watching the sun as it crested the sky. All around me were ruined flowers, piles of them that had been painted in a green-colored substance that ruined the petals. I could have left them alive, given Conner and his hive a much-needed break, but I was being petty, and the scent of this many peonies only served to remind me of the night he took me in a bed of their silken petals. It had been romantic, sensual, and perfect. I fucking hated it, hated their rich aromatic scent, the feel of their soft stupid petals, everything about them pissed me off now.

"You know we could just open a flower market and make a killing selling these things." Laura snorted when I glared over my shoulder at her. "You need to talk to him. You've been going up to the roof just to feel closer to him for days now. Listen, I get it. It is a fucked-up situation on both ends, and neither of you saw it coming. I personally hate him, but I hate him because his breathing hurts you. You're my best friend, the one I call when I need to hide a damn body. We've had each other's backs since I pulled you out of that heap of trash you'd sat your skinny, terrifying self down on. I know you too. I know you're hurting to go to him, and you won't. You are you, and the most stubborn witch I have ever met. You have spent your life helping broken things find a home and a coven, two things they never would have had without you. You turned this broken-down shithole into one of the world's top academies for spoiled assholes to pay for the coven and their needs. You could be the Queen of the Witches if you only reached for it, and yet you don't because you love him. You still love him, and he loves you. There's literally only you and Conner standing between your souls uniting. Choose love, Avery. You're worth it; you're worth so much more even though you can't see it. He saw your scars, and he's still here. He is trying to get your attention, and so what if it is to say sorry. Let him say it and see what happens from there."

"You think I don't know that? My issue is this: what if I let him, and it's a goodbye? What if I can't accept that? Worse, what if he doesn't want me anymore and I have to learn to live without him again?"

"What if you never take the first step to figure it out? What if he still loves you and wants you back? What if we stopped using what-ifs and just figure it out? The entire world could end tomorrow, but that's tomorrow, and this is today. He's here, trying to talk to you, and you're so fucking broken that you can't see it because the idea of being hurt again is terrifying. It's supposed to be scary, Cheveron. It's supposed to terrify you. It's your forever, and if he says goodbye, it will be goodbye. Tell me you don't want him, tell me that and I will be at your side to search the entire world for a cure to cut the ties between you. Tell me, and we will go right now and do it together."

"I can't say it," I uttered as I bent down, lifting up a single flower as I brought it to my nose and held it there. "I know I love him still, and yet I know we can't ever be what we were. We've changed; we're no longer the carefree children who thought they could take on the world. We wanted to make the world a safer place for both of our races and change the laws of them. He did that without me. He changed the laws and did everything we were supposed to do, and he did it without me. I'm afraid that even if he can forget the scars I hide, the pain I've endured, what would we do? Everything we'd meant to do together has been done."

"You make new plans," she said as she watched me closely, knowing me as well as I knew her. Centuries together had done that, and we were closer than sisters. "I am hunted, you know that. What you don't know is, I'm bound by the mating of souls like you are. The man who hunts me, he is my soulmate. He's done more than I care to admit, and I carry those scars with me. I've killed him in every rebirth he's had. He is mortal, and yet he isn't. He comes back every time, and every time, he's worse than he was. He's a storm within me that I crave more than I crave the air that fills my lungs or the magic that dances within my soul. Braydon is my bane, and my salve, and every fifty years, he returns to me, and I'm forced to kill him. We're cursed, and he becomes infatuated, and everything turns dark. When it turns dark, it becomes a choice between my life or his, and I choose mine to go on. I have to watch him die, the man I love more than air, and I watch him die by my hand. I know your pain, and I understand it well, Avery. Unlike my story, yours has a chance to be rewritten again. I know you, and I know you love Conner, because no matter how hard you try to ignore that ache, it only grows worse as the time passes. You are the sun, and he is your moon and stars. Think about it before you ignore a chance at happiness. Some of us are cursed to remain unloved, while others ignore their chance. Of all the things I wish for you, your happiness is first and foremost. I'll leave you to the flowers, but at least keep a few of them. I find their scent most soothing, sister mine."

Hours later, as darkness descended and the light fell behind the mountains that surrounded us, I stood upon the roof in a maxi dress that exposed my shoulders and had slits cut up to my waist. The wind blew around me, howling as it rushed through the valley. I felt him before I caught his masculine scent. He didn't speak as he stood behind me, didn't move or ruin the solitude of the serene setting in which we stood. Exhaling deeply, I let my soul brush up against his, needing the connection as he waited for me to turn around.

He hadn't brought anyone else with him this time, and I almost felt sad that they weren't planting more flowers below. Laura's words echoed through my mind, and I knew if given a chance, or a choice, I'd run from this moment. I feared his rejection, knowing I'd been used as I had, well, he'd liked my innocence and I had none of it left. I carried that proof within me, the amulet may have hidden it from the world, but I had lived it, and now he knew it too.

His hands slipped around my waist and he pulled me back against his granite-hard muscles. His nose touched my ear, and I closed my eyes and relaxed into his touch. Still, he didn't speak as we stood there, basked in the light of the moon.

"There is something I need to show you, imp. Something I found long ago and have kept hidden from the world. Will you come with me?" His voice was deep, sending a ripple of desire rushing through me.

"I shouldn't," I uttered as I turned around, searching his eyes as he held mine. I waited for the disgust to pass over his features, for his eyes to shift from mine. He did neither. Instead, his mouth lowered and brushed against mine and a moan of longing left my throat. "Conner," I moaned huskily, needing him with everything within me.

"Come with me, and if you want, you can leave at any time you choose. I won't ever force you to stay, Avery. You are free of me and my kind should you choose to be."

"You think you could hold me there against my will? You think I'd trust you after you treated me like shit and allowed me to be abused? You have some pretty big balls coming here, let alone asking me to do shit for you."

"I think I'm an asshole, but I lost everyone, Avery. I lost you, and it damn near killed me to think you'd turned against me willingly, and that I had allowed our enemy in to murder the King. I thought you had turned against me, and murdered my entire hive to teach me a lesson. I have spent every day since believing that. I didn't hurt you. If I had felt you didn't want to fuck me, I wouldn't have forced you to do so. I was an asshole, yes, but I made it clear that you were under my protection while you were within my stronghold."

"Addison didn't get the memo, nor did you when I expressed that neither Clara nor Laura were to be harmed. I played the part you wanted me to, and I did it only to keep them safe from harm. You broke the terms when Clara was harmed, you're just lucky she doesn't carry the same scars that I do, or I'd be the monster you think me to be."

"I was with you when she escaped," he countered as his voice dropped an octave, and he held out his hand for me to accept it. "I killed the vampire who broke the law and harmed her. I am the King, and my word is law. I am not my father, Avery. I am not the little boy who stood in the shadows and watched you touching your innocent flesh, knowing I was there. We are not the same people, but this thing we share, it is forever. There's also the thing I need to show you. Come with me, and I'll have you back here before the sun rises over your pretty mountains."

"Fine, but I'm not playing whore for you anymore. I've played that part enough, and I don't enjoy it much at all," I whispered and placed my hand into his, hating that the moment I did, sparks flew between us. I could feel his heart racing in perfect symphony with my own; feel his need rushing through him as violent as my own, responding to his single touch.

We were like two opposing storms building, both vying for dominance as we ripped across the land. He pushed, and I pushed back. One touch and we forgot the past and the pain, and the world faded to blackness around us. I knew better than to allow this, to let him touch me, and yet the moment he pulled me closer to him, it was me who stepped onto my tiptoes and brushed my lips over his as I whispered his name, like he was my savior and not the man who had handed me off to his family to be tortured.

It was like ice-cold water had been splashed over my face, and I paused, shoving him away from me hard enough that he moved. "You *left* me! You left me to those monsters, and they ripped me apart as I begged them to do it! I was awake when your father fucked me and used his metal claws on my back as he took me in front of the hive. I begged him to hurt me, to destroy me because he'd given me *your* blood. You were my downfall, Conner. A single drop of your blood mixed with mine and I did whatever they wanted, even allowed them to flay my flesh open as he fucked me. My back, I can still hear him slicing through it as I begged him to fuck me harder, to rip me apart more!"

Tears filled his eyes and his throat bobbed as he watched me crumbling. His hands lifted and then dropped as if he'd wanted to hold me as I hugged my stomach. He couldn't argue it now, and the ugly truth of what had happened to me was just that: ugly, violent, and brutal.

"I couldn't feel you. I felt nothing, and to me, it meant you were safe. I thought maybe, just fucking maybe the universe had taken pity on me and broke the unnatural bond between us. I didn't know you suffered, or that you were being harmed. I trusted my father to protect the one thing I loved most in this world because he'd given me his vow as King, but also as my father.

He was supposed to protect you, and he took you and fucking wrecked you instead. I can't ever make up for what happened, nor can I ever go back and undo it. If I could change the past, I'd have taken you and run from them, from the world."

I threw myself into his arms, not because his apology was great, but because I felt the truth of his last words in my soul. He meant it, which meant he hadn't known what his father had planned to do with me. I wanted his arms around me, even if only for a moment. I wanted him to wash away the memories, and his touch did that. To me, that was everything. Those demons I carried, they chased me, haunting my dreams and every waking moment since I'd returned from reliving it and recanting my tale to him and the others.

His mouth touched the shell of my ear, and I moaned as he held me. He didn't force a kiss or ask for more than he felt I wanted, and that allowed me a moment to just forget. My arms wrapped around his neck as I whispered against his ear. "Take me to your bed, and make me forget his touch, Conner. Just tonight, please?"

"My pleasure," he growled, pulling me with him, as if he was afraid I'd change my mind. And I could with the cold, horrid memories that plagued my mind these days. For months, I'd woken up covered in sweat as memories of his father had wrecked any chance of sleep I had. "Hold on, little waif," he whispered and picked me up effortlessly, as if I weighed next to nothing, and jumped from the academy's roof the moment I had wrapped my arms around his neck. "I'm going to make you forget the pain you endured, even if it means giving up my crown and walking away from this place. I'm going to erase everything that ever happened to you and replace it with me."

"I'm not sure that is even possible," I returned as my voice broke. Tears slipped from my eyes as he rushed through the woods with his inhuman speed, zigzagging through the trees until we breached the barrier where his land started and mine ended.

"Challenge fucking accepted, little witch."

CHAPTER SEVENTEEN

I thought I was prepared for him, but Conner wasn't kidding when he said he would erase the memories. We entered his mansion through a secret entrance, and guards blocked the doors that led into the hallway we used. They didn't as much as glance in my direction as we moved past them. Once we were in the living quarters, I found it vacant of life as he hurriedly tugged me behind him.

Once we reached his room, he stilled and turned, pulling me into the room with him as I closed the door behind us with my magic. He smirked, his eyes lighting with laughter and I didn't balk or back down. He, on the other hand, paused.

"Wait here, please?" he asked gently, his eyes searching mine for something. Rejection, maybe? I didn't know what he expected, or what I had by coming here, other than the obvious. I guess I hoped that he wanted me, to be able to look at me knowing my scars and see me as he once had, as something still beautiful.

I watched as his hands left mine, and the euphoria

of his touch escaped my grasp. My heart rose to my throat, wondering if I'd been too hasty by coming here. He turned, staring at me as if he'd felt the direction of my thoughts.

"I need it to be perfect," he explained. "I need you to trust me, Avery. I just need a moment." He disappeared into the bedroom, and I leaned against the door. My mind screamed to leave, to escape this place and the vampires within it, and yet I wouldn't.

Seconds after he'd vanished, the heady scent of flowers touched my nose. A glow came from the bedroom, and I stepped away from the wall, drawn towards the creature that had held my heart for centuries. At the threshold of the bedroom, I paused, knowing that I held control of what happened next. I held control of what I allowed to happen to me. I was in control of my life and my destiny, and if I chose to allow him back into my world, into my life, there had to be trust between us. I stepped back, breathing harshly as I considered if I should move forward, or if I should turn and run, but I collided with something solid against my back and spun around, coming face to face with Conner.

"Scared, little witch?" he asked as he grabbed my hand and held it against his heart as it raced uncontrollably fast against my palm. "I'm scared too because, to me, you are everything," he admitted. "I'm terrified that you will run or reject me."

"And I'm afraid you will never see me as I was. I showed you my scars, and you know my secrets."

"Your scars were caused by my choices. You are fucking perfect, and even if you didn't use your amulet to hide what happened, I'd still love you. I have loved you from the moment I pulled you out of the pile of bodies you lay within. I didn't understand it, not at first. I wanted to hate you, and yet I couldn't. I craved this little girl, one who had yet to bloom into her radiant beauty or womanhood. I felt like the worst kind of monster for wanting you when you weren't old enough to understand it, but I knew what you'd become.

"Then I watched you grow into your beauty, and I craved you, imp. I craved you so fucking much that no matter how hard I tried, or what I told myself, I would end up in the shadows of your room, watching you bathe as you became a woman. I watched you touching your innocent flesh and whispering my name as you came, and I wanted you more than the blood that sustained my life. I took lovers just so you could watch me, so that you'd know what I wanted to do to you. Yeah, we were fucked-up, but there was magic working against us. You were created for me, and I don't know what I did to deserve something so perfect and innocent, but I wasn't about to question it," he said as his thumb lifted to my cheek, rubbing away the tear that trailed down it. "You are my soul, my first and only love, Avery Cheveron. I have never known anyone else in my entire life that has ever made me feel like I do when I am with you. You make my heart race, and my soul lights up around you. No one else has ever even begun to fill the void you left in my soul. I am not perfect, and I have made many mistakes where you are concerned, and yet you still choose me to keep your monsters at bay, even though I have become one. If you walk away, I will watch you, and I will stand aside if it is what you desire, but if there is even the slightest fucking chance of getting you back,

I'm willing to fight to make it happen."

I lifted onto my toes and pulled his mouth to mine, kissing him deeply with everything I had in me. I gave him me, all of me in one kiss that pulled a moan from both of us. He smoothed his hands down my back, hooking them beneath my legs as he lifted me, hoisting me up. I wrapped my legs around his waist and let him walk us towards the bedroom.

Inside the room, he paused, holding my body against his before he turned us, and I pulled away from his hungry kiss. He'd lit candles, hundreds of them around the room until they heated it with their dancing flames. Petals floated over the water of a bath he'd filled, while the bed was covered in flower petals.

"Bathe for me, imp," he uttered, and there was a hint of worry in his tone. I stared down at him from where he still held me up.

"I will bathe for you, my prince," I whispered thickly, caught off guard by his fear of rejection. "Will you watch me from the shadows?" I asked, knowing he wanted to play his game with me; predator versus the vulnerable maiden who was unaware of death creeping in the shadows.

"Always," he answered as he sat me down and pulled me in for a long, hungry kiss that had me teetering on my feet, then released me. "Touch yourself and whimper my name for me, and I will make it weep to come when I fuck it with my mouth."

With that, he left me standing alone, fighting to make my lungs remember how to draw air into them. He moved away from me as I turned to face the bath, knowing his position without having to look for it. I could hear his turbulent heartbeat as it raced. I could sense his soul as it reached for mine. Once he vanished into the shadows, I removed the dress I wore, slowly letting it drop to the floor in a rush of silk fabric as the predator watched me from the darkness. My panties followed, and I reached for the hairband he left beside the tub, slowly lifting my hair to expose the curvature of my neck for him. Slipping into the tub, I exhaled as the water touched my flesh, soothing the anxiety that threatened to reach up from the pit of despair that was always just below the surface.

I used the richly scented soap, slowly lifting my leg to wash the length of it. When I'd finished cleaning my flesh, I dropped the soap and let my fingers skim over my supple skin as a moan ripped from my throat. I leaned back, dropping my legs open as I touched my aching cunt, pushing my fingers through the soft, silken petals while I pictured Conner doing it instead of my clumsy fingers that didn't fulfill the need rushing through me. I moaned his name, pushing into my flesh as the heated water bit against my skin. I was lost in what I was doing, no longer able to hear his heart beating over the sound of mine roaring in my ears as the orgasm threatened to send me reeling over the edge. His hands touched my neck, turning it as his fangs sank into my throat and the orgasm turned into a bomb that ripped through me, tearing my body to shreds. I used one hand to hold his mouth to me, while the other continued touching my flesh, driving the orgasm to a painful point where it became too much.

His fangs withdrew as he pulled me out of the bath, lifting me up, he walked me backward, soaking wet, to the bed and lay me down upon it. He stepped back, staring down at me before he knelt on the bed, kissing the inside of my thighs as he slowly climbed my body. His hands curled under my thighs, trapping me to his mouth that lowered and held me to the bed. His tongue snaked out, dragging through my slick folds as a moan built in my lungs, exploding from my lips as he devoured me. He licked from one end to the next, using his nose to apply pressure to my clit until I was bucking against him with my hands, helping to hold him where I needed him most. The room spun around me and I whimpered his name over and over, repeating it like a mantra as he climbed up to rest between my legs, which fell open in invitation.

I stared up at him, watching as he used his thumbnail to cut through his lower lip. I knew on instinct what he was silently asking me. I felt a moment of panic, knowing that we'd become unhinged if I allowed this to happen, and yet he was asking to know what it was like. To become mindless together through the blood that combined from us.

"I need to know what it is like, what it was like for you," he uttered. I chewed my lip, sucking it between my teeth before I sliced through the thin flesh and watched his eyes turning crimson as the blood dripped down my chin and rose to sit before him.

"Close your eyes," I whispered as I captured his face between my hands, needing to build enough courage to plunge into this insane idea with both feet. I watched his thick, black lashes flutter closed and I pushed my nose against his. "I don't know what will happen, but I was mindless, and everyone I touched became you.

Somehow, it made it easier for me. I'm not certain what will happen when both of us do this, Conner. Don't hurt me, please." I leaned forward as his eyes opened, sealing my mouth against his as our blood ignited and rushed through us both.

The room faded away, and his hands grabbed me, lifting me onto his cock as he drove his erection deep into my flesh. I screamed as my eyes opened and I stared at his image, crystal clear, his aura exposed around him as he stared back at me, then looked down where we were joined as one. Black wisps of magic ran up his legs and torso as crimson red wisps rushed up mine. I moaned as his hands rocked me, using me to conduct the wisps of magic that rushed through us.

"It's beautiful, this wild magic we create together, my beautiful sweet witch," he groaned as he lifted me, slamming me down until I was panting as sweat beaded from my brow, rolling down my breasts while the heat of the room consumed us. "This is what souls mating together looks like, isn't it?" he asked as he watched me place my hands on his chest while golden hues of flecks covered anywhere I touched. It was as if we'd taken acid and were stuck in some lucid hallucination together.

I felt his need to drive into me hard, painfully, to erase the pain of what I'd endured with pain that brought pleasure. I could hear his heart beating, dancing in tune with mine as our bodies created magic that was so wild and intense that I wasn't sure I could survive it.

"Conner," I uttered as the first sensation of the orgasm began to glow inside of me. His eyes lowered, watching the lights that built inside of me as the candles were extinguished around us. We glowed together; the magic that worked from our blood seemed to be growing. He pushed me back, spreading my legs as he drove his cock into my body deeper, harder, unable to control the need to pleasure my body, my soul. Conner's mouth crushed against mine, claiming the scream as he rocked his hips. When he pulled away, his eyes were violet, hunger had faded, and yet his fangs grew, and his mouth moved to my throat. The moment they sank into my throat, the light exploded and I detonated. My cunt clenched his cock, milking his own release from him as he continued taking from me until finally, he stiffened above me. His fangs withdrew, his tongue slowly slipping over the cuts he'd made, kissing my neck as he lifted and stared down at me.

"I love you," he uttered as he stared into my eyes. "Marry me, Avery. Become my Queen and rule at my side."

CHAPTER EIGHTEEN

I sat beside the bed, staring at Conner's sleeping form as my thoughts collided with what he'd asked of me. It had been hours since he'd fallen asleep as the sun rose, and yet I hadn't tried to murder him or escape. Of course, I didn't want him dead, and I wasn't his prisoner, and yet I hadn't moved from his side. Eventually, I climbed back into bed, touching his skin to watch where my hand turned his skin golden even though it was growing weaker with every passing moment as the blood was diluted.

It hadn't been as it was with the others. I hadn't felt the need to do whatever he'd wanted. I did what I wanted with him, and he'd done what I had needed. We'd done it together, aimed at pleasing the other until our souls had danced with a magical sound that only we heard. My hand touched his chest, listening to it beat with mine. Any moment and he'd wake. Already the sun was setting behind the mountains. I leaned over him, brushing my lips against his as I watched him coming back to me from his eternal slumber. His eyes opened, and he rolled me onto my back, staring down into my eyes with hunger.

"Molesting me as I sleep, naughty imp?" he asked with his tone heavy from sleep.

"It wouldn't be the first time I did it, now would it?"

"Are you flirting with me?" he asked, watching me, searching my face as if he expected me to reject him, and I wasn't sure if I would or not yet. I didn't know what I wanted or how we ended or began.

"What are we doing?" I asked, and watched his smile fade.

"I don't know, but I know I need to see where it leads us. Last night bound us deeper together, and it felt right. I know you felt it because I was inside of you. I knew what you wanted, what you needed, and I wanted more than anything to give it to you."

"I know, because I did everything they wanted because I felt the need to please you, and to me, they were all you," I said as I pushed him away from me and sat up. "I need to leave."

"You're running from me, my sweet witch." His eyes watched me as I chewed my lip, uncertain what to say. I loved him, and I always had. I wanted him, but this man had left me, and it had broken me. I wouldn't survive that again, not when he held my soul in the palm of his hand.

"Not you, us. I'm running from us, Conner. I don't even know if there is an *us*, or if there can be an us. I'm not even sure how to be me most days, let alone to let you back into my world. I'm a mess, and I don't know how to move from where I am emotionally right now. I have clawed my way back from the pain and the torment I suffered, and I made a life for myself, one where you weren't the center of my entire world." I paced aimlessly before him, moving back and forth as my mind whirled with what I wanted, and what I needed. "I like who I was before you came back into my world because I felt as if I served a purpose and now that is gone too. I help others who are or have been in a similar situation as I was. It's a lot to deal with when I've spent years hiding from you, and now you want me back, you want what we had, and so do I!" I screamed the last part and paused as he smiled with heat burning in his eyes. "That came out wrong."

"I think we want the same thing. I know it's a lot to take in, and even for me, I'm not sure how we make this work now. I do know I want us, and I want it to work." He pulled me into his arms, tipping up my chin as he stared into my eyes. "The thing is, there's more that you don't know. Something I just discovered recently myself, and I'm not sure how you will feel about it once you find out. Hell, *I'm* not sure how I feel about it yet. I do know that I need you to confirm my suspicion, and I need you to trust me."

I narrowed my eyes on his as my hackles rose. An uneasy feeling filled the pit of my belly as I nodded to him. Whatever it was, it couldn't be good. I could feel his inner panic, sense his own uneasiness as he nodded to a pile of clothes that had been set out. I wasn't even surprised it was a dress, but I was surprised that it was mine, and one I'd worn centuries ago to lounge about his room.

"Where did you get this?" I asked.

"I kept it, because it was one of the only things of

yours I had left. I thought maybe someday you would wear it again."

I struggled against the emotions those words created and frowned. "To have me murdered in?"

"To keep you in," he shrugged. "I couldn't kill you. I knew it when I found the remains of my family. I knew then, no matter what you had done, you would never die by my hand, and therefore, you would never leave this world as long as I lived."

"It's almost sweet, other than the part you're hiding. The part where you keep me as your sex slave to use me when you wanted," I pointed out in an accusing tone.

"It was a good idea in my head. I doubt you would have stayed that way for very long, considering I was having a hard time staying mad at you in the little time I had you here. I wanted to curl you beside me and hold you more than I wanted to fuck you. I just wanted to feel you near me again, and to smell your hair after you'd bathed." His fingers pushed through my hair, moving it away from my face before they lowered, stroking my bare arms.

"I do smell pretty good after I bathe for you, don't I?" I smirked as his eyes danced with laughter.

"Saucy wench, you always did have more sass than was healthy for a little imp."

"Go big or go home, right?" I whispered as that uneasiness entered him again. "I think you should show me what you're hiding. It doesn't seem like you think I'll be happy with it."

"Out of everything the bond gives us, I don't enjoy this one, or at least you knowing what I am feeling."

"But it would be fine if you could feel what I feel,

isn't that a little one-sided?" I asked.

"I didn't say it would be fair," he whispered as he watched me dress, his eyes noting the way the amulet glowed as I exhaled. "What does it do for you?" he asked when he noticed me watching him.

"It is powered by ancient magic, and needs a vampire sacrifice every full moon," I said as I lifted my head, watching while his eyes narrowed and I smiled, giving away the joke as I watched him shaking his head. "It's spelled to hide damage of the flesh. Laura figured out a way to make it work, and we now make them for women who have been battered or carry scars. We offer them the amulet, and in return, they help someone else who has been harmed."

"Come," he said as he finished slipping his shirt on and held his hand out.

I followed him with my hand in his, allowing myself to feel the connection for a few more moments. I thought we were heading into the main hall, but he turned, taking me down a winding staircase that led into the basement. On the stairs, I paused, pulling on his hand as fear ripped through me.

"I give you my oath as King that I will not imprison you or do you harm. You are under my protection while in my lands. You're safe with me, Avery. Come, she waits for you."

"She?" I asked.

"Come, I can't tell you, not here." He pulled on my hand as he squeezed. I started forward slowly.

"Conner," I said as another wave of fear sliced through me. "Lights, please," my voice broke as I whispered it and he turned again, noting the sheen of sweat on my brow. "I'm not good with dark holes or dungeons in general anymore."

"Use your magic, little witch. This part of the mansion isn't protected from it."

I exhaled and lifted my fingers, calling forth a flickering flame that lit the staircase before us. My hand slipped back into his, and I inhaled before letting it escape slowly. He waited, watching me as I struggled through the anxiety and fear that slowly left.

We made our way down to the bottom level where Mayhem and Addison both waited in front of a large opulent door. They wouldn't meet my stare, and for once, I didn't blame them. One had relived my horror, while the other had played an unwilling participant. To Mayhem, I stepped closer, forcing him to look at me.

He swallowed audibly as he lifted his eyes to meet mine. "Avery, I didn't know I was spelled, or that I helped them. I mean, I knew it was either your life or Conner's, and I chose my brother. I should have realized it was magic when I tried to tell him what happened to you. I should have felt it."

"You didn't have a choice, and I knew that. If you'd have ever asked me, I'd have told you to protect Conner. Grigori would have had him murdered if you had betrayed him for his son. I know, because it was what kept me in line. If I had attempted to escape and failed and was captured, he would kill me and Conner both. If I escaped, Conner would pay for my crime. He had us both unable to fight him, so when I felt the darkness within me stir, I held onto it. I forgive you, Mayhem. I'm glad you listened when I warned you to leave and protect him. Hemlock was a master in deception, and even I failed to feel his spells." My head lowered, sadness spreading through me as the memories roared to the surface once more.

"You killed them all, and my only regret was not being there to help you. I didn't mourn them, but I also couldn't tell him that I had helped them to make you into what you became. I loved you like a sister, and he wanted me to rape you. He wanted to watch me as I took you. It made me sick just hearing him say it, and I wouldn't do it. I also couldn't seem to make him stop; it was as if he was under the influence of magic, which makes me wonder if we weren't all part of Hemlock's game, under his spell the entire time." He shoved his hands into his pockets and frowned, his eyes lifting with regret filling them as he watched me.

"I remember," I whispered thickly. "You left, and I destroyed them all. I'm glad you didn't rape me so that I didn't have to murder you too. I also have begun to wonder if there were more spells in play, which lifted upon Hemlock's death."

"Me too, because if you had raped her, you'd be dead right now," Conner growled while his eyes turned black at the mere thought of it.

"I didn't hurt her, ever. I pretended to, and she screamed like I did. I told her that you were safe and that she would endure the torture and survive. I did what I had to do to protect you. You're my brother," he uttered as he clasped Conner on the arm. "She made me promise to keep you safe, even when she was drugged, she protected you. I couldn't tell you, not because of the magic, but because I couldn't save her from it. I could only sit there and watch as they tormented her. I have lived knowing what she endured to survive, and it fucking haunts me. You were crowned King soon after you woke from the slumber, and you couldn't be told the truth. You'd have lost it, and I knew that. My only goal has been to guard you, and watch your back, as I promised her."

"It's over, let it go and remain in the past," I whispered thickly as Mayhem nodded, and Conner's dark eyes swung to me as he agreed.

"Are you really going to show her without warning Hope first, Conner?" Addison uttered, irritated. As if she feared something or was trying to protect whatever lay on the other side of the door from me.

"Avery needs to know. She deserves to know." Mayhem folded his arms, staring at Addison as if he would rip her head off if she dared to argue it. "Explaining it first won't change anything. It's easier this way."

CHAPTER NINETEEN

66 "I need to know what?" I asked, watching as Conner swallowed hard. This couldn't be good. He stared at me, watching me carefully as he began to speak.

"I returned to my father's keep to find nothing but death. I thought you'd killed everyone. I was grieving; grieving the loss of my family and thought that I'd led a wolf into our house, one whose sole intent was to destroy us. Inside the servants' living quarters was a small babe, maybe a year old at most. I told Addison to take her into London and leave her at the steps of the orphanage. It was then I noticed she carried the magic of the witches within her and I changed that plan. I intended to murder a child because my grief was too much to bear, and I wanted the blood of every witch who lived. Addison moved to do as I commanded, to take the child to the throne room where I would end her life. But the babe, she turned and looked at me with blood-red eyes. In my grief, I missed it, what lay right in front of my fucking face.

"She was of two bloodlines, witch and vampire,

and since my father had kept multiple witches in his keep, it never even clicked into my mind what she was, or who she might have been. I only knew that she was an abomination under the laws of that time. We hid her from the world, never allowing her to see the skies, or know the world outside of this mansion. I couldn't kill her after I'd learned what she was because she was something you'd fought for, and it reminded me of you and your endless challenges you gave me. It kept you and your dream alive for me, which made me fight harder to change the laws. Months ago, when you showed me your scars, when I looked at your stomach and figured out what they had taken from you, I knew." He shook his head, as if he was seeing my flawed image. His dark eyes lifted with pain filling them as his head tilted to the side. His mouth tightened, as if he felt pain for what I'd endured. "I knew when I saw what he had done to your stomach that you'd been pregnant when I left you with my father. We think he heard her heartbeat within you, and Mayhem confirmed that something about you drove our father mad to the brink of insanity. You were locked into the pit in the dungeon for months after that. You were spelled to sleep, and what you thought was mere days was actually much longer. Mayhem said you vanished for months, but not enough time to carry a child to term," he swallowed, fear showing in his eyes. "I think he tried to kill my daughter, *our* daughter. Instead, I think he realized the rarity prize he held and left her alive. She is the first child born of Hecate's line to ever mix with another breed other than your own. She's a Cheveron witch, one of immense power who is immortal. I believe she's our daughter, Avery," he said softly, his voice shaken as if he was afraid to say it too loudly. "I think I've held our own child locked up to protect her without ever realizing she was ours. Your blood will sense her where mine cannot. If she is ours, you will sense it through your maternal bond and bloodline."

I stared at him and everything inside of me denied it. "I wasn't pregnant," I whispered breathlessly.

"We were being spelled; we were manipulated before I ever handed you over to my father. What Hemlock said was true. I felt the need to breed with you, but worse, in the month leading up to my decision to save you, I gave in to the magic that I felt pulling me toward you. It wasn't the bond we shared that I felt; it was the need to create a life with you, one whom neither of us actually wanted, but magic made us think we did. I wanted you to grow round with my child, and to create one to rule the world. I never wanted to rule anything, which should have made me think twice about the insanity of my thoughts. I didn't. I watched you drink tea that was laced with fertility spells knowing what it was, and every night I fucked you deliberately so we could create a life. I couldn't stop myself, which I now know was because I was spelled to breed with you. I know it is true because, with Hemlock's death, those memories were freed in my mind."

I gaped at him as I turned towards the door, eyeing it. I'd wanted to be a mother. I'd wanted Conner to create a life with me, even though it was forbidden. I hated that we'd always been so careful, but his words drummed up memories. Memories of the frenzied sex, the need to consume the tea that tasted like shit and yet I'd drank it every night. Afterward, I'd stripped bare and taken him over and over, and could never get enough of him. Not that we'd needed to be spelled for that part, but the way it happened, it made more and more sense.

"Open the door," I whispered. I wasn't waiting around for more stories, not when it would be such a simple thing to walk through the door and whisper one sentence. "Does she know about me?" I asked with wide eyes as everything inside of me screamed to see if we'd created a life together.

"No, she only just learned that I am her father, and I wasn't sure you'd ever come back here. I didn't want her to feel as if you'd reject her if you rejected me. She is not safe from the covenant, not without both her parents standing against them. I may be the King and have an army at my back, but having a Cheveron witch at my side would stop them from even thinking of coming after her."

"If what you say is true, you'd have three Cheveron witches at your side, and over one thousand forgotten witches."

"How is that possible, unless you rose to be Queen and kept it hidden?" he asked. "Wait, three?"

"I am the Unspoken Queen, and I do have a coven, Laura leads it. I back her up. She is also a Cheveron witch; she's the one who found me because my blood called her to me. She was abandoned, cursed, and left to die, so she hid who she was until she found me."

"Jesus, it's like it is raining Cheveron witches lately," Mayhem said with a whistle. "Shit just got exciting."

"Open the door," I whispered, and when they hesitated, I used magic to reach around them and open it myself. I entered silently, staring down at the witch who held her hand up, catching an ancient tomb in mid-air, singing with earbuds in as she went about what she was doing, oblivious to our entrance. She seemed young, as if being locked away had somehow made her evolve slower, and yet by vampire standards, she *was* young. But she was also a witch, and that was unheard of for our kind, and yet here she was. Her hair was tied up into a makeshift bun which was held with a pencil. She was petite, as I was, and had features that were sharp and yet delicate at the same time. Violet eyes the color of Conner's studied the pages of a grimoire that was yellowed with age. From here, I could read the lines of the spell that moved over the pages. The leather bindings of the book told its story, and yet she didn't seem aware that what she held was a living, breathing thing that held pieces of the soul from the witch who had written in it. "Blood of my blood, see me," I uttered barely above a breath and my heart clenched as those pretty eyes turned and took me in. "Blood of my blood, feel me," I whispered again as everything inside of me called to her as the bloodline linked, and our bond became solid. "Holy fuck," I cried and my eyes pricked with tears as I took in the child, I'd never even known I'd had. She looked at me like I was a stranger, because to her, I was.

She withdrew her earbuds and stared up at me as she slowly rose from her chair, defensive as she felt the same thing churning through me. "How the hell did you do that?" she demanded with wide, panicked eyes.

"Blood of my blood, come to me," I whispered again, watching her body jerk forward as she struggled to fight it. "Daughter of mine, I command you to heed my words, come to me." It was the words my mother had used on me when I refused her or ignored an order. She started moving, and everything inside of me broke open as the last of the bond slipped around my heart, telling me she was mine. A sob escaped my lips and Conner moved to me, wrapping me in his arms from behind as he stared over my head while our daughter walked up the staircase to us with an irritated glare.

"Hope Halverson, meet your mother," he whispered over my head. "Avery Cheveron, one of the oldest and most powerful witches alive in the entire world."

"I thought you said you didn't know who my mother was. I look nothing like this one. Maybe we should get your ancient ass some glasses, Conner."

"Language, ladies do not cuss unless the situation calls for it," I whispered, and she stared at me pointedly.

"I don't fucking…" her mouth shut as I whispered the words in my mind.

"I do not care for swearing among ladies when we are having a civilized conversation. Should the need arise to swear, we will both do it. Now, I am Avery Cheveron," I said as I pulled myself together while my eyes burned with unshed tears. "I am your mother. You carry my blood in your veins. The spell I spoke, it only works on direct descendants of my line, which I assure you, you are, as there are only two Cheveron witches alive who could have carried you, but only one was sleeping with a vampire with those pretty violet eyes you inherited."

"Then maybe you can explain why you ditched me, why you never cared to stick around, so someone knew who I was."

"I didn't ditch you, Hope. You were taken from me before I ever knew you were alive. I just found out that you existed five minutes ago when they told me right outside of those doors. I never knew I was even pregnant with you. God above, I wanted you before that, but life isn't easy. It doesn't give you what you want; it gives you what you need. Normally at the wrong time, or for reasons we don't understand, but stronger forces are normally driving us to what we need. Rosemary," I said as I stared at her and then down at the grimoire that had revealed the next ingredients she would need to work her spell.

"What?" she asked as she chewed her gum and popped a bubble on purpose, staring at me. I eyed Conner, wondering what he allowed her to do since he'd hidden her from the world. She seemed young, but I knew differently.

"She's been very sheltered, and I probably shouldn't have allowed her endless YouTube use, but she had limited options in this age." He shrugged as she popped another bubble, which drew his eyes to her with ire. She was popping the bubbles because it angered her father. I almost laughed, but the pain in my chest was real, the tightening around my heart as I stared at her profile grew worse by the moment, and I knew I was about to make an ass of myself by crying in front of her.

"The spell you are working on calls for rosemary, but not any rosemary. It needs to be blessed by the moon and the sun. You are using another witch's grimoire as well, which is dangerous as it carries the taint of the last witch who used it. Can I assist you in the spell?" I asked with nervousness that I shouldn't feel, but did, and she stared at me for a moment. My favorite time of childhood had been with my mother, learning her craft with her. I'd had that time stolen from me with Hope, and I could teach her more than any other witch alive if she wanted me to, and I prayed she did.

"I guess that would be okay," she shrugged as she spoke. "I don't get many witches down here other than Luca, and he doesn't think I should be learning certain spells. I enjoy the craft, but I'm aware of it being something someone should be taught correctly." She pulled out the gum and watched me with the same wariness I felt. "Are you doing this because you want to, or because you feel obligated?" she asked.

"I really want to teach you," I whispered. "My mother taught me for a time, but then she was unable to teach me more. I wish to teach you as she did me."

"And if I ask you to teach a certain spell that Luca said shouldn't be done, would you?" she countered.

"Such as?" I asked as I followed her down the stairs, feeling Conner's eyes on us.

"I wanted to make a boyfriend, but he wouldn't give me a corpse to reanimate. I'm two hundred four years old and have never been kissed before. I've been hidden from everyone, it makes dating kind of hard, and a girl has needs."

I choked on the air at her words. "Luca is correct on that one. That's some pretty hairy stuff that is against the laws of the universe and carries a very high cost to use. You don't want to mess with necromancy, not in a mansion full of the undead. I mean, it's a pretty dangerous spell." She hadn't been kissed? It explained her immature attitude and attire, but also her defensive attitude towards me. She feared rejection or what we would think of her, but if she'd been hidden away from the world, alone, it made sense.

"I'm a pretty powerful witch," she said softly, staring at me as we reached the grimoire.

"You would be, as you carry my bloodline and I am the granddaughter of Hecate."

"Really? Oh, my Gods that is unheard of! That means if I am your daughter, I have it too! I've read so much about her down here, she's amazing, and we're from the same bloodline, are you sure?" Her wide eyes showed her excitement, and my heart flooded with warmth as I struggled to speak past the tightness of my throat.

"Yes, I'm very sure of it. It also means you shouldn't bring back dead things to date. I will be getting you out of here and into the world soon enough that dating won't be a problem," I informed as I gave Conner a sideways glance to see if he would argue it. "There are rules we follow, rules meant to protect us. What is dead should always remain dead unless they're undead."

"I'm guessing you weren't really into rules, considering I exist." She watched me as my lips twitched. I gave in to the urge and smiled, watching as her eyes widened. "I have your smile and dimples."

I stared her mouth and swallowed hard as I nodded, then she smiled to show me. "So you do, but you look an awful lot like my mother. Your eyes, of course, came from your father, which should have told him whom you belonged to a long time ago. Your hair isn't the same shade as his though. My mother had black-blue curls that she could never tame and more often than not, wore them like yours is now. She had this perfect heart-shaped face that I wish I had been blessed with, and she was fierce and so strong of mind that I thought she could rule the world had she put her mind to it. She was kind, and the strongest witch I had ever met, and still have yet to meet one who matches or comes close to what she had. She was more powerful than I was, and I wished to be like her when I grew up."

"What happened to her? If you're immortal, why isn't she? Did she die?"

"She died of the plague trying to save humans from the sickness that killed thousands of them before anyone knew what it was. Before we knew or understood the sickness that killed them, we went into a sick house and were infected with the plague."

"I'm sorry, that had to suck," she said as she sucked her bottom lip between her teeth and considered her words carefully before she spoke again. "Weren't you in a coven with her? If she went in, why didn't you go too? Aren't covens supposed to do everything together as one?"

"I did go in with my mother, my entire coven did. One by one, I watched them die, and then I burned them and gave their souls back to the leyline from which they were created. That is how I met your father; he saved me. He brought me back to life, and we created you together."

"And you lived happily ever after?" she snorted sarcastically, knowing it was anything but a happy ending, all things considered.

"For a while, it was a fairytale, and there were beautiful things we shared, then I was tortured, ripped apart by an entire hive of vampires, including your grandfather, the King of the England Vampires, and I survived until I ended up here again, prisoner to your father. Now here we are together again," I said, clapping my hands together.

"I think I'm going to need some vodka and popcorn and the rest of that story to understand how we ended up at this point. Did you say my father held you as *his* prisoner? No wonder he pled the fifth about who my mother was. I need the tea, so spill it."

"I don't have tea?" I said as she smiled wide and shook her head with a cheesy grin on her face.

"Addison taught me that tea means drama or secrets. Really, I'd love to hear the truth of what happened, and how you lost me. I've longed for a mother and father, but I never dared even dream I had them. Auntie Addison taught me a lot of stuff, like how to get drunk, or how to kill someone three hundred different ways from Sunday, but you're my mother and my father, and I know we just met, but I feel you inside of me. I'd like to know more about you both."

"Sit with me, and I will clear up what I can, but it isn't a pretty story, Hope. It's dark, and not entirely something that even we fully comprehend, yet," I said as Conner came to my side, and I felt his uncertainty. I turned, staring at him as something inside of me heated, and the reality of what stood before me really hit me. We'd created life; a life that was forbidden by the covenant, and they'd come for her. He reached for my hand, slipping his fingers through mine as he brought it to his mouth and placed a soft kiss against the back of it. The panic seemed to be swallowing me, even with his hand holding me and giving me strength. We'd broken the covenant, and the penalty would be her death.

"Not with us at her side, imp," he said confidently. "I'd rip their throats out as you melted their flesh from their bones. *Our* daughter will never know pain as you did, and she will never face persecution under their laws."

"That doesn't sound good." Her words registered in my mind as I turned, staring into her pretty blue-violet eyes with a fierce need to protect her from the world. No wonder he'd kept her hidden, even from me.

"They'll come for her." My tone was soft, yet tight as everything inside of me fought to be unleashed to keep her safe from the outside world.

"They don't know she's even alive. Only those at the trial heard Hemlock, and most think he was insane."

"They already know," I whispered. "And they're coming."

CHAPTER TWENTY

I stood inside of the academy's main hall where we fed the students during the day and then trained at night to avoid the vampires. Today, there was a chill in the air, a bad omen that something was coming. The last time I'd felt it, I'd ignored it and ended up as Conner's prisoner. Today was different; today he stood beside me as I placed the crystal quartz around the room, preparing a spell to make the entire school vanish to anyone who looked for it with the intent to do harm. Hope was with me, her eyes wild with wonder as she took in the witches who worked as one, helping me with the magic I used. She was a sponge for knowledge, and I almost hated Luca for having been her first instructor, but he'd gladly stepped aside and was now learning my spells with us.

I had a daughter, one who looked like her father. I'd joked with Conner about him missing it since she was her father's daughter. Her black-blue hair clung in lovely waves today, falling just short of her ruffled skirt and shirt that said Anarchy in red, with droplets of what I assumed was blood dripping from the scrawled *A*. Her heels clicked along the floor as we watched her. She was vibrant and unafraid of the outside world that viewed her as they had once viewed me, a rarity and one-of-a-kind creature.

"I can't believe you're a mother," Laura whispered in a hushed tone beside me as she took in the beautiful girl who explored with her wide, violet-blue eyes searching the entire school for anything and everything.

"Me either, but I feel her. The moment I whispered the bloodline spell, I felt her within me, as if she was a part of me. She's powerful, scarily so. Young though, probably because she's been sheltered for so long," I said with a shrug. "We will teach her what she needs to know, as family is supposed to do."

"That is something we can worry about after we've made it clear that our daughter is not to be touched nor hunted by either race. I have sent a message to the Vampires that live in the Cascades in Western Washington. Brandt has agreed that he will back us and protect her should others come to argue it. He will stand with us should we need him. I don't think it will be needed, but I'm not sure how many will come to argue her life. My question is this: how the fuck did they know she existed? I've kept her a secret since the moment her pretty little eyes turned red," Conner said.

"It was a spell; that must have been what was unleashed when you killed Hemlock. I felt it, but I wasn't sure what it was at the time. I'm guessing Hemlock put something into place in case she had survived the hive's death. He more than likely had something in place in case he died prematurely to let the world know what we had done. It's like a death note, one that releases upon their death," I said as we started towards the door with the others following closely behind us. Outside, the sky was foreboding, gray, and filled with a starless night.

"Hope is a hybrid Cheveron witch. She is a born vampire, to one of the few lines who can still birth them. This will draw them to her, but it will also give them pause before they try to destroy her. She's as powerful as you are, Avery, and as strong as Conner. She can and will handle herself against those who seek to harm her. You made a hybrid." Addison looked at us pointedly, as if we should be proud even though her words said the opposite. I almost wanted to hate her for having taught my daughter anything, but I was glad Hope had someone to teach her.

I stared at Addison, realizing she wasn't wrong with what she said. We had created a one-of-a-kind child who held power from both of us. My head tilted as I listened to the tune of the magical song that danced on the wind, as if the entire area was protected by wind chimes. They were closer to us than we expected.

"We must go, now," I uttered as I moved towards where Hope stood. "Hope, it's time to go."

"We shouldn't run," she said, stopping me short of reaching her.

"We're not running. We are preparing to face them," I replied. I couldn't explain to her that a strategic battle plan was better than a half-assed one, we didn't have time. I opened my mouth to speak as a bolt of magic sliced through the air, aimed at Hope. I moved, taking her to the ground with me as I shielded her with my body. "Stay down."

"No, they just tried to kill me!" she seethed and

pushed at me, her magic rearing to life as if she held it shielded as I had. Her eyes turned crimson, while her fangs lengthened with her anger.

"Blood of my blood, stay down and go to your father," I growled and let my power radiate through the clearing. Her eyes widened as I stood, letting every ounce of power I controlled fill the air around us. Static raised the hair of the coven members who stood closest to me as Laura moved into place beside me, letting her magic skim against mine while they combined and, one by one, the coven gave us their strength and we stood, facing the witches that threatened my daughter and all of us. Crystals of all color glowed around the field as the witches entered it, staring at us through a hatred born of fear of the unknown. Prejudiced bitches needed to get into this century already.

"Avery Cheveron, you are charged with treason and the murder of Roger," Margaret hissed as she pulled her power around her. Her hands glowed with immense power, poised to throw it towards us should the need arise. "You also broke the laws of your time, creating a monster that should never have breathed her first breath."

"Did you just call my daughter a *monster*?" I asked as I smiled at her coldly. "I'd be cautious with your next words, Johor," I uttered, using her surname and line in disdain.

"I am two hundred years old; when you speak my name, you will say it with the respect I deserve. I am the highest-ranking member of the coven in the entire state of Washington. I am more powerful than any other around these mountains."

"Except for the three Cheveron witches before you, that may be true. However, seniority goes by age, does it not? A Queen is chosen by her power and age, and I *am* the oldest witch present." I watched her, letting my words sink in while her anger rose.

"You wish to be Queen? A vampire whore? The only way you can take my position is to end my life, and I assure you, Avery, you never will!" Margaret hissed as she raised her hand to strike me with her magic.

Laura's hand rose to block the spell as mine lifted, calling for her flesh to wither. My lips moved as our coven behind me began chanting, and as I watched closely, her body begin to shake in pain as water was pulled from her flesh. It was the same spell I'd used on Grigori; that I'd used to slaughter an entire hive of highly trained ancient vampires. Her mouth opened and a scream tore through the meadow. I didn't move, didn't twitch as I focused my energy into consuming hers as her companions watched helplessly from the shadows where they had hidden. Her eyes rolled back in her head, her skin turned to a husk, and the wind carried her magic to me on a gentle breeze as I consumed not only her magic but her insides to heal the damage that had been done to mine. It was how I healed, how I was able to remove a little damage, and yet I'd never wished to take from my sister witches until now. I consumed her, healing my womb and the damage to my internal organs that Grigori had done when he'd ripped my daughter out of me.

The entire field watched in stupefied silence as I consumed her ashes until nothing remained. My fingers turned black as it crawled up my arms from where she healed me while I consumed her through dark magic. It sucked her dry, turning her to mere ashes that wafted on the wind and entered my body through the points she healed. The moment it was finished, I turned to the others who had come here with her.

"My daughter is not a monster. There are no laws that state she shouldn't be alive, not anymore. Should any of you feel differently, speak now. I am Avery Ilsa Cheveron, the oldest witch in this state and Queen by right; I have lived among you as the Unspoken Queen, silently leading you from the shadows for over two hundred years. I have chosen to remain uncrowned and have now murdered your Queen. By right, I can ascend to her throne, and none of you could argue it," I uttered hoarsely as my body adjusted to the power I had just consumed.

"You will never lead us! You are tainted by him, your lover for whom you whored," Joffrey seethed. I moved space and time through a single whisper of magic and the air filled with the scent of coppery blood as he looked down, where my hand was pushed through his chest and had ripped out his heart. The entire field erupted into chaos as vampires faced witches, and witches met them head-on in open battle from opposing sides. I watched silently as Conner took the head off one witch before he spun, slashing through another, who crumpled at his feet.

My eyes viewed the blood, the gore, and then landed on the last witch who had yet to fall. She was powerful, and yet she seemed immune to the death of those who fell around her. The moment I started forward, her green eyes held mine.

"I do not wish to engage you, for I am not here to demand you surrender. I am here to crown the victor of the battle. If you kneel, I will crown you Queen, Avery Cheveron." Her eyes glowed from within, power exuding from her, and I stalled before her.

I turned, staring at Conner and Hope, who both watched me with pride. They had no idea what it meant to be crowned Queen to Witches. I shook my head as my heart squeezed with what it would mean for them if I accepted it.

"Laura Aria Cheveron will be crowned Queen of the Witches," I said, hearing Laura's sharp intake of breath. "I cannot be Queen, because I am in love with a vampire. I choose him. I choose love. I will not wear the crown that will stand between us in all things. Laura will be Queen, and I will stand beside her, ready to defend my Queen should the need ever arise. This is my oath, bound by the blood of my blood, and sister of my soul. I relinquish my right to rise to Queen and forfeit it at this time to someone better fit to rule us," I whispered thickly as I turned, finding Laura's eyes wide with horror as I kneeled to her. "Rise, my Queen," I said through a smirk as laughter danced in my eyes.

"You're an *asshole*, Avery."

"You knew whom I would choose, and you are the only one fit to rule us. You will make a fierce Queen, and your decisions will be based on what is best for the coven as a whole. I cannot make that promise. I love Conner, and I am a mother to a vampire who carries my bloodline. I will always choose what is best for them, and that is not something the Queen can do. You are strong enough to do this, and I will be at your side every step of the way. We *all* will be. I spoke to the others before I made this decision. I didn't make it lightly. I love you as my sister; you know that. I would never be able to give my whole heart to the coven, as Conner has had it since the moment he saved me."

"I'm really mad at you, so stop making my heart ache, asshole. I accept, but on the condition that we create a coven that is one with the vampires. I want a united hive that allows us to live as one. I want a place where those who are broken and hurt can seek shelter and find sanctuary. I want a world in which both will accept your daughter, and create a new, better world for her to live within. That is my request to ascend to Queen, Avery. Yes or no?"

"I don't know if I can . . ."

"Agreed, but only if you do me the honor of being my wife, and become my immortal mate, Avery Cheveron," Conner said from directly behind me. I turned, finding him down on one knee with a delicate, silver band that had once belonged to my mother held between his fingers. His eyes searched mine as he waited for my answer. "I don't know what the future holds, but I know I don't want to live in it without you. I can't ever take away the pain of the past, or the shit I did when I thought you had betrayed me, but I do know I want to try. I want you; I've always wanted you since the moment you whispered my name and tried to protect me from the sickness that ravaged through you. I love you, imp. I love you so much it fucking aches. Marry me. Marry me, and be my Queen and rule at my side."

"Yes," I whispered through tears that choked off my words.

Conner rose from the ground and held me in his arms as he kissed me before every witch and vampire present. His hands smoothed down my back as he rested his forehead against mine.

"I'm going to love you until the sun burns out and this world dies around us. Even then, I will love you from this life into our next, my soulmate."

"Does this mean I don't get two Christmases?" Hope asked, and we turned, staring at her. "Mayhem said if you guys didn't hook up, I would get twice the presents."

"She takes after you," Conner uttered against my ear.

"Pretty sure she takes after both of us, which is way worse than just one of us."

"Wait, witches will live *with* us?" she asked excitedly and started jumping and clapping her hands as if she were a child.

"Eventually, but there are many things that need to happen before it can be arranged," Conner said softly. "First, I have to marry your mother before she changes her mind."

I smiled at him as something slithered over my flesh. My smile faltered and I turned to stare at Laura, who frowned as she watched me with a foreboding stare. "Did you feel that?" I asked, and we both looked up at the sky as the moon was blocked out by darkness.

"Something dark is coming," she said.

"Something evil is in the air," I agreed.

"Darkness is falling, and no one is safe, you must come to this very wicked place." We turned, staring at Hope who watched us through black eyes. The glyphs that covered her bare shoulders pulsed with power and I frowned as she turned, staring at the moonless night. "Come one, come all, it's time to gather at the ball. There are hexes in the air for those who care," she whispered. As we watched, her eyes turned back to violet and she frowned. "Something wicked is coming; what will you wear? Choose it carefully, for you may find more than hexes to be dancing in the air."

"Hope?" I whispered as she shook her head and smiled at me.

"Is she a seer of darkness?" Laura asked as she moved to my daughter, placing a hand on her shoulder, and her eyes turned white as she saw what Hope had just seen. "No, not evil," Laura groaned. "It's way worse. I've been summoned to the Witches' Ball in New Orleans through Witch Radio, which apparently happens to be your daughter, somehow. Something is trying to warn us against it though, as if there were clues in the invitation. I must call the western side of the state and see if Brandt is aware of it or has felt the darkness in the wind. He and Claire have been very helpful in the last week, even with everything they have going on, and other issues they've had to deal with."

"So, we don't go then," I offered. "Not if something is trying to warn us against it."

"I'll go," Laura stated as she brought her hand down and turned to me. "It's not a request that we attend; it's a decree that all covens send at least two witches to attend it as representation. I am the newly appointed Queen, and I have been personally summoned to attend it. I will go. You can hold the coven down and deal with whatever the hell he is speaking about. I'd rather not be saddled down with paperwork anyway. Payback is a bitch, Avery," she said with a sassy smirk lifting her lips.

"I think I can handle paperwork," I said as I studied my daughter's slumped shoulders. "Hope needs time to get to know her aunt though, and with everything here being mundane and up in the air, you could take her with you. Get to know your niece and show her around to those who will accept her."

"I don't think that's a wise choice," Conner injected, his hands reaching for mine as he shook his head. "You just said there is darkness in the air; she's our daughter."

"Addison is right; Hope is both of us, Conner. She is stronger than you think she is and carries a very powerful bloodline in her veins. You and I will smother her light trying to protect her; it's a given. She is our daughter. But she has to get out there and spread her wings, and she also has to be allowed to show the world that she is a force of nature, one who won't be fucked with. We can't do that for her, only she can. Laura is the second strongest witch alive, second only to me. She will protect Hope, and it's a ball for Goddess's sake. How dangerous can it be?"

"She knows little of our world, other than what she's learned on YouTube or the internet," he argued.

"She's two hundred years old and has never been kissed. You can't just step in and be her father, no more than I can just become her mother. You also can't stop her from growing up. Besides, I don't plan to let you out of bed for at least a few weeks. Let Laura take her and send Mayhem with them. Lord knows he will scare off anyone stupid enough to try to touch our daughter unwantedly."

"Are you serious?" Hope asked, and I turned, staring at Laura, who smiled at me.

"I'm honored that you trust me enough not to fuck up your daughter, Avery. I'd be honored to take her with me to the Witches' Ball. I won't even talk mad shit about her father while we are away," Laura said and scrunched up her nose as Hope flung herself into her arms. "You must get that from your mother," she chuckled as Hope bounced from foot to foot, excited.

"This is amazing!" she beamed as she started towards us and hugged us both as we placed our arms around her. I stared at Conner over her dark head and smiled as tears swam in my eyes. "I don't care about the past, or what happened, but I am glad you're my parents. I am also happy for you both, and glad you're putting it all behind you and will be getting married. You both deserve to be happy."

"She gets that from me," I said with an embellished wink to Conner.

"She got a lot of things from you, imp. Her astounding inner beauty and diversity is something I will never argue over because it's what made me fall in love with you in the first place."

"Is now a good time to tell you that I stole a womb?" I whispered and Hope stepped back, making a grossed-out face as she back pedaled towards Laura, who stood away from us with the coven, going over her plans for New Orleans.

"You stole a what?" he asked.

"I took a womb so that we can try again. Johor was allowing hers to go to waste, and I want babies with you. I want my forever with you. I don't care if we're immortally hexed, because as long as I have you, nothing else matters. I want a son, one who is as brave and strong as his father. I want you. I want everything back that was stolen from us, and I want to start trying for a son right now. Let's not wait or waste time. Let's start our forever right now."

"I love you, sweet witch. I don't know how you can forgive me, or how I will make up for what happened to you, but since you're immortal, I have plenty of time to do so."

"I don't need you to do anything other than love me. Take me home, I need to bathe, and then I need you to make love to me. I love you, Conner. I've always loved you, and I always will."

~The End~

WICKED HEXES

Wicked Hexes is coming in October 2019, Laura's story!
Make sure to stay tuned in the Midnight Coven group for
updates on all exciting things Coven related.

ABOUT THE AUTHOR

Amelia lives in the great Pacific Northwest with her family. When not writing, she can be found on her author page, hanging out with fans, or dreaming up new twisting plots. She's an avid reader of everything paranormal romance.

https://www.facebook.com/authorameliahutchins

http://amelia-hutchins.com/

IMMORTAL PROMISE
VAMPIRE MATES
KIM LORAINE

I t's been close to seventy-two hours since my life was changed irrevocably. I walked into a coffee shop and laid eyes on the woman meant for me. Like a scene from a Greek tragedy, that was the same moment she'd been brought to death's door. I've spent three nights waiting to see if I've done what a mate should do for his woman—save her. No matter the situation, my instinct screams for me to protect, defend, and claim her. My eyes burn from the effort of keeping them open as, once again, I feel the sun begin to rise even from the safety of my home. I will not sleep until I know she is mine.

"Brandt, Elaine has transitioned. This one is a lost cause," my friend and fellow vampire Mattias says.

A growl builds in my chest. How can he expect me to give up so easily? "Stay out of this. You have what you want. I can sense the spark of life in her."

He approaches, and I shoot him a glare that would wither a lesser man. "She's gone. You can't stay here like this much longer."

"I'll do whatever I have to in order to serve her

when she rises."

Letting out a sigh, Mattias places a hand on my shoulder. "I am taking Elaine back to my clan at sunset. She's still in the haze of her transition, but soon she's going to ask about Claire. I have to tell her the truth."

Claire. My mate's name is like a stake through my heart. All this time by her side and I never knew. I run a finger over her pale cheek. "Claire," I say, testing out the feel of her name on my tongue. I want to say it and have her eyes flutter open, for her to offer me a smile, for her lips to utter my name as well.

"I must tend to Elaine. Please, consider what I said, Brandt. You need rest."

I shake off Mattias' hand and return my aching gaze to Claire's eerily still form. "Safe journey."

I feel it when he leaves the room, and soon my eyes are too heavy to keep open, the sting in my blood feeling more like fire. My lids slide closed, and all I know is darkness.

* * *

"Where the ever-loving fuck am I?" A woman's voice shakes me from my rest.

I bolt upright, gaze trained on the brunette in my bed. "Claire," I breathe.

Her eyes widen, and she backs up, clutching the sheet and pulling it up to her chin. "Who are you? How did I get here?" Then her memories must flood back, because she turns the color of bone and lets out a cry as she touches the now healed wound across her neck. "He…he slit my throat."

"Easy, love. He's gone. Never to harm you again." I reach my hand out, but she flinches away.

"Everything hurts. It's so…loud in here."

"It's your transition. You must feed before you'll feel as you should."

"I…feed?"

Slicing open my wrist with my own fangs, I offer her my blood. "From me."

"Fuck you, asshole. Is this some kind of twisted game? I'm not drinking your blood."

"You will if you want to live." I know instantly that was the wrong thing to say. Her eyes show nothing but fear in their depths.

"What happened to Laney? Where is she? Let me go. Please. I won't tell anyone where you live. I promise."

"Claire, your cousin is fine. Her mate turned her and saved her life."

"I…I should be dead."

I shake my head. "You're a vampire. You're transitioning because the man who attacked you slit your throat, but I saved you. I turned you. But you have to drink now or your body will reject the change. You'll be truly dead."

I stand over her, holding my wrist close to her lips. I know I've got her when she inhales through her nose and her pupils dilate at the scent of the blood. She licks her lips, and my fucking cock goes rock hard at the sight of her pink tongue darting out of her mouth. I could force her, use my power to transfix her and command her to drink, but I won't. She needs to do this of her own free will.

"I don't want to be a vampire," she whispers.

"But you don't want to be dead either."

Her brow furrows. "No…I don't."

"Drink, my mate. Then we'll move through this together and come out on the other side."

A soft whimper leaves her, but she leans forward, and her mouth brushes my skin. Then her fangs latch on to my wrist and she drinks deeply. Pure pleasure races through me. Not only because of the rush of need that hits me at the feel of her, but because of the soul-deep satisfaction of serving my mate. This is what all the stories couldn't explain. *This* is why my clan stopped searching for our mates. The feeling can't be taught. Seeing is believing, and now that I have her, I fucking believe.

She tears her lips from my wrist and gasps, a small line of blood trailing down her chin. I reach out and wipe it away with my thumb. I want to kiss her, claim her, make her mine in every way.

"My mate," I whisper.

"You keep saying that. I'm not your mate. I don't even know your name."

"My name is Brandt. All you need to know is, you're mine. My responsibility. I made you a vampire, I'll protect you forever."

She backs away and holds up both hands. "Hold on, Casanova. I'm a big girl. I can take care of myself."

"You cannot."

Standing, she cocks a hip and rests her hand on the gentle swell. "Yeah, I can. Thanks for…saving me and all, but I'm out of here."

I intercept her in two quick steps. "I'll not risk your safety. You are my mate."

I put my hands on her shoulders, but she jerks free of my grasp. "Don't touch me."

This isn't how our union is supposed to go. She should want me as much as I want her.

She glances around the room, then down at her blood soaked clothes. "Where's my purse? My keys?"

"I'm sure they're still at the coffee shop. But, Claire, you can't go back."

"Why not?" There's venom in her eyes to match her voice.

"Because you'll kill the first human you come across. You'll decimate this little town and then spend eternity unable to live with yourself."

"And I suppose you're the only one who can keep me from turning into a monster?"

"No, but I am the right one."

She laughs, but the sound is bitter. "Then get me out of here and teach me how to control myself. But after that, I want you to get the fuck out of my life."

My gut clenches, but I nod. This woman is going to be the end of me. I'll win her heart. After all, we have eternity.

www.books2read.com/immortalpromise

Printed in Great Britain
by Amazon

40653254R00137